THE UGLY CHRISTMAS SWEATER

JACKIE PAXSON

CONTENTS

OTHER WORKS

Tabloid

This is for you, Dad. Christmas Mornings aren't the same without you.

Cover Design: pro_ebookcovers.

Proofreading: Rosalba Ugliuzza

Interior Formatting: The Write Designer

First printing, 2019.

Any references to historical events, real people, or real places are used fictitiously. Names, characters, and places are products of the author's imagination.

CHAPTER 1

Squeaky rodents sang about Christmas over the speakers of the coffee shop. Christmas had come early to Two Beans and a Latte. Two Beans and a Latte had been my primary job since I was in high school. Being a thirty-two-year-old barista was never my plan. Thankfully, the owners Sean and Dean let me continue working there after college when the event planning jobs dried up.

Sean and Dean were two of the greatest people I've ever met. Sean was the typical tall dark and handsome guy. He drew attention from both men and women when he walked through the shop. Dean attracted his own attention. With his blonde locks, he looked like he'd be at home in California.

They fit together like two perfect puzzle pieces. Two Beans and a Latte was their dream. Together they had built a customer base that loved them and their quirky ideas. Their dedication and love for Two Beans was the main reason I tolerated their need to celebrate ALL holidays.

Each holiday the shop had to be decked out in every decoration possible. Staff have to wear holiday-accented aprons and hats. Windows are covered in lights, garland is hung throughout the shop, and each holiday has its own play list. The music is played on repeat until you're dreaming about it at night. Christmas has the best variety. The Easter playlist was painful. A person can only hear the bunny hop so many times before wanting to jab their eye out with a spork.

Thanksgiving had just ended, and Christmas had thrown up in Two Beans. Dean was spraying fake snow on the windows while Sean followed behind him applying window appliques. I tied my turkey themed apron, pulling my hair back in a low ponytail and putting on a brown hat that said gobble, gobble.

"Why are we decorating so early?" I walked over to the door and flipped the sign from closed to open.

"Oh, darling, you know I just love Christmas." Dean winked at her.

"Yes, I know, but it isn't even after Thanksgiving." I whined.

"It's close enough. You should be happy I am not making you wear your Christmas apron and hat yet."

I clenched my jaw while I wiped the counter off.

Sean walked over to the counter. "I know you aren't the biggest Christmas fan, but I gotta do what the boss tells me." He shrugged.

"Boss? I kinda like that. As long as one of you knows who is in charge here." Dean said sassily while adjusting a garland he hung.

The bell tinkled over the door. Meg, a slight middle-aged woman, hurriedly rushed in. "I'm sorry. I'm sorry. The bus was late." She ran in like a whirlwind. In her rush to tie her apron, she nearly tripped over the garland laying on the floor. Stuffing her hair under her hat, she started brewing the coffee I hadn't started yet.

"No worries, hun. Cierra had it all covered." Sean picked up the end of the garland and draped it over the counter.

"Ok good. Sorry, Cierra-" she apologized. Then in a whisper that Sean and Dean couldn't hear, "Did I miss him?"

"No. I just flipped the sign a few minutes ago."

"Good. He's the highlight of my day."

I crossed my arms and stared at her. "You have a boyfriend."

"A girl can look. He is good to look at." She smiled.

The man in question was a regular. He looked like some high-powered attorney, CEO or billionaire. He wore Armani suits clearly tailored to him, expensive Italian shoes, ties that were impeccably tied, and expensive cuff links shone every time he handed over his money.

Dirty blonde hair always had the just had incredible sexy look. A chiseled jaw and slightly crooked nose gave him the look of a runway model. It was his blueish grey eyes framed by long lashes that melted a woman's panties. If you add in his deep phone sex voice and his elusive smile, you had a god among men.

"Excuse me." A deep voice shocked me out of my daydream.

"Oh . . . uh . . . sorry." I stuttered.

My daydream was staring at me with a slight grin. "I want a coffee black with one sugar."

"Yes, sir. Anything else?" A blush crept up my neck as I avoided eye contact.

Looking down at his phone, he absently answered. "No"

He handed me his black Amex card without another word. My reaction to this man was the same every day. All it took was a smile then I'd turn into a blubbering idiot. "I will have that right up for you."

Before the words left my mouth, Meg handed me his coffee. "Jay." I called. With a confident swagger he walked over and took his coffee with a sexy smirk. He walked out the door letting a cool breeze into the shop. The tinkling of the bell jarred me out of trance.

"I hate to see that man go, but I love to watch him walk away." Dean sighed.

Sean elbowed him while Dean just shrugged. "I can appreciate a work of art."

"Preach!" Meg threw her hands up.

"I have to say though; my favorite time of day is when he comes in." All heads snapped toward Sean. "What?"

"At least I try to pretend I don't like seeing him come in every day." Dean crossed his arms.

Sean laughed. "It isn't that, hunny bunny. Cierra gets all tongue tied and stupid around him. In all the years, our sweetie has worked here, she has never done that. It's quite entertaining."

I blushed for the second time in five minutes. "Ugh! You guys suck. You're the worst friends and co-workers." I marched to the supply room to get cups we didn't need

An hour later, the shop was bustling. People came in and out of the shop for the Two Beans coffee and pastries. Pastries were provided by the Tattooed Tart. Dean's sister, Dinah, owned it. Dinah was most sought-after pastry chef in town. She happened to also be one of my best friends.

Dinah Rhoden looked nothing like her brother. Dean had an athlete's body. He was well muscled and clean cut. He could easily pass as a male model. Dinah was curvier, had sleeves of tattoos and an attitude that made anyone think twice if they wanted to mess with her. Her hair was in a pixie cut and usually dyed an ostentatious color. She changed it according to how she was feeling. If they made a mood ring hair dye that changed with her mood, she'd use that on a regular basis. Currently, her hair was bright pink tipped in black.

Coming from the back, Dinah carried in fresh sweet-smelling treats. She took her time arranging her fresh muffins, honey buns and scones. Meg and I worked around her while she placed them in perfect order. When she finished, she walked over to the coffee and helped herself to a cup.

"Dinah, I'm going to start making Cierra charge you for that." Dean remarked.

"Oh, fuck off, big brother." Dinah shot him the bird.

"Dinah!" He reprimanded.

She sighed and looked at me while I finished ringing up the last customer. "What?"

Dinah smirked. "You, me and Katrina still on tonight?"

"Of course. Why wouldn't we be?"

Shrugging, Dinah said, "Never know if you two might find dates someday."

I snorted. "That ain't happening."

"I was hoping you finally grew a pair and asked out Mr. Man Candy."

I stuck out my tongue. She laughed and moved to leave. "We are meeting at The Cellar at 6, right?"

"Yep."

"Ok. I will see you there." She walked across the front of the shop and stopped. She stared at all the Christmas décor and grimaced. "Dean, it looks like Frosty the Snowman took a shit on your window.

Were you blindfolded when you were decorating because that's the only excuse for this hot mess."

"Dinah! Leave!" Dean yelled. Dinah laughed barely audible over the now blaring Christmas music.

Some days, I really hated my job.

CHAPTER 2

The Cellar was the perfect dive bar. It was dark, sold cheap beer and great chicken wings, and had karaoke night once a month. That was tonight. Dinah, Katrina, and I come at least a few times a month, but we make sure we come here for this mayhem.

"Hey Cierra!" Donny, the bartender, handed me my beer.

"Hey Donny. Have any contenders tonight?" I asked, angling my head towards the girl now singing an off-key version of Taylor Swift's *Bad Blood*.

"Not yet. The girls meeting you here tonight?" He served a drink to the person standing next to me.

"Dinah and Trina should be here soon."

He nodded. "You better go get a table. I'll make sure to stop over when it slows down."

"Ok." We would be seeing him again soon. He had a huge crush on Dinah. She wouldn't give him the time of day. Trina, on the other hand, only had eyes for him, and he was clueless. My friends were a hot mess.

The next karaoke disaster took the mic when Dinah and Trina came waltzing in. Dinah waved to Donny behind the bar. Trina avoided eye contact and blushed. I shook my head and waved them over to the table.

"Did the ding bat take our orders yet?" Dinah asked about the new waitress, Ashley.

"Not yet. You shouldn't say that too loud. You know she is Donny's cousin."

"I can say it how I like. I don't give a damn who hears me. The girl has the brains of a walnut."

"Try to be nice tonight." Trina snapped.

Dinah sighed, "I come out here to relax. Not have all these damn rules placed on me."

"Hi ladies! What can I get you tonight?" Ashley asked with her high-pitched voice.

"Beer and wings." Dinah barked.

Unfortunately, Ashley's attention was now on the stage. "Ooo . . . I love this song." She proceeded to sing along while standing at our table. Dinah looked at me and gave me an "I told you so look".

"Ashley!" Donny exclaimed next to the table. "What did I tell you about singing and dancing by the tables instead of taking their orders?"

"Uhm . . ." she blushed and looked at the ceiling. "If you want to dance and sing by tables then go find a job at the Booby Palace."

"Exactly, so take these ladies' orders and get back to work."

Ashley asked what they wanted again. Writing it down this time, she sped away as fast as her clear-heeled wedges would carry her.

"Clear heels?" I said.

"She totally wants to be a stripper. She'd fall off the pole the first day though." Dinah pointed out with certainty.

"Sorry, ladies. I swear it's like herding cats with her." Donny watched his cousin get distracted on her way back to the bar. "How are you, Dinah?"

Dinah kept her gaze pinned to the stage while she waved her hand.

Hurt flashed over his face, but he quickly recovered. "Your food should be out soon. Let me know if you need anything else."

I watched Donny walk away.

Donny wasn't a bad looking guy. He was built like a bouncer and had dark wavy hair with brown eyes. His face was rugged with a permanent five o'clock shadow. He was a bartender at night but during the day he counseled troubled kids. I never understood why Dinah wouldn't want to go out with him. In this town, he definitely qualified as a catch.

"Why are you like that with him?" Trina asked Dinah.

"I'm not interested, and he doesn't need to think I am. He needs to go ahead and notice you mooning over him." Dinah said, stealing a sip of my beer.

"Hey!" I slapped her hand.

"One of these days I am just going to tell him to ask you out, Trina." Dinah said.

"Don't you dare." She quickly looked around.

"What? Don't act like you wouldn't want that to happen."

Trina sighed. "I want him to ask me out because he finally sees me. Not because my obnoxious friend tells him to."

"I understand." I patted her shoulder.

"Good because I have a favor to ask you." Trina said.

Trina's "favors" were never a good thing for me. But, I asked anyway.

She looked down at the beer Ashley had set down in front of her. "Will you come to my company's Christmas party with me?"

I did a full body cringe. I've gone with Trina to her company's Christmas parties before. Last year, one of her co-workers puked on my shoes, another groped me, and a third nearly set me on fire by trying to light his cigarette while trying to lay on my chest. "Um. That's gonna be a hard pass for me."

Dinah laughed. "Trina, why did you even ask? Cierra almost becoming a Roman candle last year should have clued you in."

"It didn't happen that way. He was trying to be cuddly and forgot that you can't light cigarettes while laying your head on someone's chest."

Dinah and I looked at Trina like she'd lost her mind.

"Come on, Cierra. I promise this year will be fun. It's an "Ugly Sweater" party." She wiggled like a puppy that needed to be let outside.

That sounded horrible. "I don't know."

"Ooo . . . she's crumbling." Dinah egged Trina on.

"Why don't you take Dinah?" I asked.

They both gave me "what have you been smoking" looks. "I don't think that's a good idea."

"The last time I went, I punched one of her colleagues."

"Sandy still doesn't forgive you for that by the way."

"I warned the bitch. I told her if she asked me one more time if I wanted to decorate a damn ornament, I was going to punch her. She didn't listen." Dinah lifted one shoulder unapologetically.

"See, I can't take her." Trina pointed to Dinah.

"Take Donny." I urged.

"Take Donny where?" He appeared out of nowhere.

"What the hell? Are you part ninja?" I jumped.

"Nope. You guys were just deep in conversation. So where do you want to take me?"

Dinah and I looked at Trina. "I have to go to the ladies' room." Trina stood and walked away.

"You are such a dumbass, Donny." Dinah turned away from him and looked at the stage.

"What did I do?" Donny looked perplexed.

"For a smart guy, you really can't see things right in front of you. Maybe you should look closer." I snapped.

"I don't understand, Cierra."

"You aren't going to until you want to."

He stared at me for a minute then looked toward the bathrooms. Shaking his head, he walked back to the bar.

"He's an idiot." Dinah said to me.

"Yes. If only he opened his eyes. Trina is such a catch."

Dinah nodded and looked back at the guy on stage singing *Do You Think I'm Sexy?* The answer to that was a resounding no.

Trina came back with red-rimmed eyes and sat quietly.

"Are you ok?" I asked.

"Yes."

"Good. I will go with you to your company party." I relented.

"Are you serious?" She brightened.

"Unfortunately, yes. But, just so you know if anyone pisses me off I'm taking a page out of Dinah's playbook and throat-punching someone."

"That's fine. Oh my God! Thank you so much. I have the perfect ugly sweater for you too."

"Wow! I'm clearly that predictable."

"Yeah you are, sucker." Dinah raised her beer for emphasis.

I raised my beer back to her.

CHAPTER 3

I was going to kill Katrina. The ugly sweater she picked was horrendous. It had a red and green plaid background with a sexy Mrs. Claus that said, "I'll be your Ho Ho Ho." I will be getting seriously drunk. The horrible sight reflected back at me made me cringe. Only alcohol would make this tolerable.

"You look great!" Trina squealed when she picked me up to go to the party.

"You're seriously the worst friend. How did you get the sweater with a llama with a Santa hat, and I get the Ho-Ho-Ho sweater?" I asked while locking up my apartment.

"Well, the llama one has colors I like better."

"Are you kidding me?" I said a little too loudly. The elderly lady, Mrs. Buchanan, across the hall opened her door.

"Cierra, is everything ok?" Mrs. Buchanan poked her head out of her door.

"Sorry to disturb you tonight, Mrs. Buchanan." I took a couple steps toward the elevator.

"It's ok, dear." She squinted through her bi-focal glasses at my sweater. "What are you wearing, dear?"

I glared at Trina then looked back at Mrs. Buchanan. "It's for an ugly sweater party."

"Hmm . . . well I'm glad you are finally putting yourself out there, Cierra." She grinned. "I need to go feed asshole. Have fun!"

I stared at Mrs. Buchanan's closed door. "Did she just call you easy, and what is asshole?" Trina had a confused look on her face. "That is a strange old lady."

"She definitely called me a hoe. Asshole is her cat. It's a mane coon that was originally called Bubbles, but his name pretty much tells you what he's like."

Trina paused before she bent over laughing.

"Yeah . . . Yeah she's funny. Let's get going before I change my mind and make you go to this lame party by yourself." The down button was already lit, so I smashed it for good measure and crossed my arms to hide the hideous sweater.

Trina straightened and walked over. "Sorry. It's just your neighbor is awesome. I want to be like her when I get to be that age."

The elevator door opened. I stepped in, pushed the lobby button, and crossed my arms again.

Trina stepped onto the elevator with a goofy smile on her face. I harrumphed and shook my head.

"So, I told the guy. Only an idiot wouldn't invest in CimTech. You know what he did then?" The partially drunk guy in a sweater with deer screwing was invading my personal bubble.

"I have no idea." I pretended to care and took a step away from the bubble invader.

"He invested, and I made him mad money. I'm just that good at my job, sweetheart." He ran his hand down my arm.

I pounded the rest of my drink and motioned that I need to go get another.

"I can get that for you, hotness."

My skin crawled as he went to take my glass from me. When I wouldn't let the glass go he grimaced. "Thanks, but I need to go to the ladies' room." Couples, singles, co-workers and strangers mingled all around. I weaved my way through them hoping that the invader would lose interest or lose me altogether.

When I was confident I'd lost him, I found a spot at the bar. Holding my glass up, I signaled the bartender for another. He knew my order already thanks to the three previous trips I'd made up to the bar earlier that evening. I glanced at my phone and saw it had only been an hour since we'd arrived.

"Having fun?" Trina's voice came from my right.

"Oh yeah. As long as I keep these coming." I held up my drink.

"How many is that?" She took the drink from my hand.

"Does it matter?" I looked at her. "I need these to deal with these douche canoes." With my hand, I waved around the room.

"I saw you talking with Rodger. He really is a pompous ass."

"That's putting it lightly. If I can just stay here with my drinks I will be a good girl. Girl Scout honor." I saluted her with two fingers.

"I'd buy that if you were actually a Girl Scout and held up the right fingers." Trina said. "I have to go mingle some more. I will be back later. Don't go anywhere, please."

With my empty glass in hand, I blew her a kiss. Trina pinched her lips together and continued to walk away.

How did that get empty again? Who cared? I waved the bartender over for another.

After my drink was refilled, I turned around and looked at all the stuffed shirts. Katrina worked at an investment firm. She was a pretty big deal in her company. She was VP of incoming accounts, which meant she had to socialize a lot at these things. I didn't understand why she felt the need to bring anyone. God knew bringing any of her friends was a crap shoot. Between Dinah and I, we usually drank a lot and risked embarrassing her. Dinah more than me but the way my vision was starting to get fuzzy around the edges there was definitely a chance I would be making a fool of myself tonight.

My glass was empty again. A little voice told me I needed to slow down. Gesturing for the bartender with my glass again for a refill helped to drown out that voice.

"You like your vodka and pineapple." A deep voice spoke next to me. The shivers it caused felt familiar.

Turning toward the sultry voice, a guy in a suit leaned against the bar. "Yep." I raised my glass.

He smiled a dazzling smile. This man was stunning. His eyes roamed over me and stopped at my chest. "Nice sweater."

"Yeah. Not my choice. My friend asked me to come with her. She picked the sweater. Apparently, she thinks I need to get laid."

He laughed. "Oh really."

"Yep." Leaning towards him, I stared at his hypnotizing eyes. "Why aren't you wearing an ugly sweater?" My words slurred a little on the end.

He shrugged. "It's not my style."

I snorted. "Whose style is an ugly sweater? I mean seriously who actually chooses to wear these if not for one of these parties or a Great Aunt Hildie who bought you one for Christmas, and your mom made you wear it even if it is itchy that you ended up getting a rash that lasted for your whole Christmas break. But you didn't choose it because who really would choose a sweater that would make your life a living hell for a week."

I took the last swig of my drink and motioned for another.

"Wow. That was terrifyingly specific. True story?"

"Possibly." I looked at his tie because continuing to look up at him was making the room spin. His tie was festive. It had a dancing reindeer, a dancing Santa, and Rudolph's nose lit up. "Your tie is festive."

He looked down and got a funny look on his face.

I grabbed the tie and rubbed the silky fabric between my fingers. With my other hand, I got my freshened drink and took a sip.

People started going out on the dance floor when the DJ started playing a 90's dance song.

"Dance with me." He paused and looked down at me. "It looks like you should probably work off a bit of that alcohol." He held his hand out to me.

I stared at it like it was a snake. I must have stared too long because he started to take his hand back. "Ok." I pounded the last of my drink and grabbed his hand, dragging him to the dance floor.

Weaving through the crowd, I bounced off of other dancers. Finding our way to the middle of the dance floor was the easy part. Getting my now-very-inebriated body to dance some what well was something entirely different. My legs wouldn't cooperate with me. The second time I almost fell over he wound his arm around my waist and ground into my ass. This, my drunk ass could do. Doing a little bump and grind with this sexy suit was easy.

Feeling his hands on my body and his growing erection on my ass had me getting wetter by the second. He leaned closer, and I could smell the scent of his cologne mixed with spearmint and whiskey. It was almost as intoxicating as the vodka pineapples I chugged at the bar.

"If you keep doing that, I'm going to be forced to take you to a dark corner and see if I'm affecting you as much as you are affecting me." He whispered in my ear barely audible over the music.

I spun around clumsily and locked my arms around his neck. "What if that's what I want?"

He leaned down and kissed my neck sending goosebumps all over my body. "You smell so good."

"So, do I." He laughed. When I realized what I said, I corrected myself. "You. So. Do. You."

He stopped dancing and linked his fingers with mine.

Pulling me across the room to a darkened hallway, he found a secluded spot and pushed me against a wall.

"How drunk are you?" He kissed my neck.

I moaned as his lips assaulted my neck. I needed more. Running my hands up the front of his shirt, I felt him flex. Oh Boy!

"How drunk are you, baby? I need an answer."

I shrugged and kept petting him.

He sighed and took my hands in one of his and lifted them over my head. OH! Maybe he is into some of that fifty shades kink.

He smiled. "I'm not entirely against it, but let's get to know each other before I show you my red room."

Huh? Oh, crap I must have said that out loud.

"Yes, you did." He nodded with a panty-melting grin.

Crap!

"Maybe I'm a little drunk." My head started to hurt from using words.

"Ok. We aren't doing anything more than this, but you can't keep touching me." The world started to spin too fast. *What the hell happened to gravity?*

"That sucks. I like touching you, but something is wrong with the earth." I said.

"What?"

"It's spinning really fast now. Like I'm on a broken tilt-a-whirl." All of a sudden, my body felt like it was rebelling.

"Are you ok?"

"No, I promised my bestie I wouldn't go with anyone, and I went with you."

He furrowed his brow. "No, you are looking a little green, pale and sweaty."

"That's a jerk thing to say to a girl."

"Do you need to go to the restroom?" He pointed to a door near us.

"I'm fine you-" I didn't get to finish because all at once my vodka pineapples wanted to make a reappearance. Throwing up all over his beautiful suit was not something I wanted to do. Unfortunately, my body didn't care.

Quicker than my brain would work, in its drunken haze, he had me in the ladies' room. Throwing up into one of the toilets, he was holding my hair back.

"Oh my God! What is going on here?" I heard Trina's muffled cry.

"I think she drank a few too many." Mr. Handsome said to my bestie.

"Cierra, are you ok?"

Before I could answer, another round of reappearing vodka pineapple reared its ugly head. After that round, I laid my head against the cool tile of the bathroom wall and moaned. It definitely wasn't a sexy moan. This was the moan of a wounded walrus stranded on an iceberg.

"You couldn't just stay at the bar and not act like a lush." Trina wiped my face down with a wet paper towel.

"Watch it. Don't wipe off my make-up. I need to look presentable to Mr. Handsome McSexypants over there." I whisper yelled and it echoed through the bathroom.

Trina stared with a blank expression. I gazed over at McSexypants. Even with puke on his pants he was making my panties damp.

"Oh, dear God! Stop talking, Cierra." Trina begged.

"Oops . . . did I say that out loud?" Trina nodded her affirmative.

He just smiled, but then looked down at himself and grimaced. Looking at Trina, he asked, "Do you have this? I need to get out of these clothes."

Go ahead and get out of them. I won't stop you.

"Another time, Cierra." McSexypants patted my head.

Dammit! Inner dialogue needs to stay inner.

"Yes, it does." Trina agreed. Then looking over at McSexypants, she confirmed, "I've got this. Go ahead and get out of here before she says a lot more than she wants."

Before exiting the ladies room, he looked back at my prone form. "See you soon, Cierra.

CHAPTER 4

*H*oly Shit! Who the hell put my brain into a blender? What the hell was that taste in my mouth, and why was my bedroom spinning? I rolled over and folded my pillow over my head.

"If you need to vomit, there is a bucket next to the bed."

I screamed. Then moaned again hold my head so that my blended brains didn't leak out of my ears. "What the hell, Trina? Stop yelling."

Now it was Trina's turn to groan. "There are aspirin and water next to you on the nightstand. I'd take that while I fix you my surefire hangover cure."

Hangover?

How much did I drink last night? I hadn't experienced a hangover since college over ten years ago.

Laying back down, I cocooned myself in my bed. All I wanted to do was stay right there, ignoring the fact that a marching band played in my head, a cat shit in my mouth and my stomach was trying to escape by gnawing its way out of my body.

When the band quieted down, I got flashes of memory from last night. The douche account manager, the hot bartender, vodka pineapples, and one sexy man in an ugly Christmas tie. His lips on mine. My hands feeling a hard-muscled chest. A familiar deep voice whispering in my ear.

Gingerly I reached for a mirror in my bedside table. The horrific sight reflecting back caused me to drop the mirror in my lap. A matted mess sat on top of my head. Mascara smudged around my eyes made me look like hungover raccoon. Last night's lipstick was smeared up my cheek like the Joker. My eyes traced lower and saw a purple spot on my neck. I gently prodded the area.

A fucking hickey.

Mr. Sexypants gave me a hickey.

What the ever-loving hell?

"Holy shit! You look like hell!" I winced at Dinah's loud voice.

"Dinah, be a little kind. I am busy listening to the marching band in my head." Laying down, I pulled the covers back over my head.

"Oh, hell no! Get your ass up! We have lunch plans today." She ripped

the blankets from me.

"Here you go!" Trina came in with a huge glass of green sludge.

"What the hell is that?" Dinah took the glass and sniffed it. Making a face, she handed the glass over to me.

"It's my no-fail hangover cure. I swore by this in college. It's been awhile since I've had to make it, but I'm sure it still works." Trina's voice was too upbeat for the time of day.

"It looks like a leprechaun took a dump in the glass." Dinah scowled.

I sniffed the glass, and my stomach revolted. "I don't think I can drink this."

"Oh, come on. Give it a try." Trina whined sitting on the edge of the bed.

"Yeah! Give it a try." Dinah had a diabolical look in her eye.

I mouthed "Fuck You" to Dinah. "Ok. Here goes."

Bringing the glass to my mouth was an act of pure will. The green sludge smelled like wet grass with rotten garbage. It went down smooth enough until I got to the first chunk. That's when my body had had enough.

Horrible green chunks landed in the bucket next to my bed. Dinah's cackling laughter could be heard over my retching. Good thing my fingers still worked. I gave Dinah a middle finger salute as I wretched into the bucket.

"Oh, Cierra. I swore this would have worked. Though, I had to make due with some of the items in your fridge." I just glowered at Trina.

After I finished, I laid back down and looked at my friends. "Kill me now please."

"Nope. Go take your stank ass over to the bathroom and shower. You will feel better, and you are coming with us to the new deli we've been wanting to try." Dinah insisted and took the vomit bucket with a grimace.

"Fine."

"Hold the phone. What is that?" Dinah pointed at me.

"What is what?"

"This." She poked at my bruised neck.

I blushed and turned away from her. "Oh! She got that from my new boss." Trina said.

"Who?"

"My new boss, Mr. Remington. He's the new CEO."

"Are you kidding me? You made out with some old guy?" Dinah crossed her arms and stared at me.

"I can't really remember what he looked like, but I'm pretty sure he wasn't old." I flopped back on my bed.

"Oh, he's not old. He is quite good looking. Everyone saw you dancing together. It was quite hot."

"Well that does it." I blurted out.

"What?" Dinah and Trina asked at the same time.

"I'm never going to another one of your damn company parties. Plus, I'm pretty sure we didn't kiss." I slammed the door on Dinah and Trina's exclamations of "No Way!"

AFTER LUNCH with Dinah and Trina the weekend flew by like an out-of-control freight train. Monday reared its ugly head with me still feeling the effects of my hangover, which included the hickey that Mr. Sexy Pants gave me. That man must have been part sucker fish. I attempted to cover the now dark purple mark with make-up. It didn't work. A scarf with dancing bunnies was my only choice.

As I pulled my Christmas apron on I stopped to check my scarf placement in one of the coffee carafes. A pair of reindeer antlers sat on the counter waiting for me. Pulling my hair into a low ponytail, I shoved the antlers on my head.

"Gorgeous." Dean walked up to the counter and fingered my scarf.

"Oh yeah . . . it's my favorite." I said in a deadpan voice.

"Hey, Sean. Come over here." Dean continued squinting at me.

"Yeah, babe?"

"What is different with our muffin here?" Dean motioned toward me.

Sean narrowed his eyes and tilted his head back and forth. I ignored them while I finished preparing to open. "The scarf." He stated.

"That's what I thought. What's with the scarf today, muffin?"

I shrugged and filled the sugar packet container.

Quick as lightning, Dean pulled down the scarf. I pulled away from him while my face flamed.

"A hickey." He proclaimed it like he was Sherlock Holmes, and he just solved an important case.

"Yeah. So, what?" Ignoring them, I continued my refilling duties.

"Do we know him . . . or her?" Sean inquired with raised eyebrows.

"I don't even know him. He works with Trina. Apparently, he is her new boss. I won't be seeing him again."

"Hmm . . .did you enjoy it?" Dean pretended to straighten the objects on the counter.

"I don't remember. I got trashed and made quite the spectacle of myself."

"Damn. I wish we'd been at that party. Sounds like a good time." Sean stopped pretending to work and was now leaning against the counter. I just shook my head.

"What party?" Meg asked.

Dean and Sean regaled Meg all about my humiliating experience while walking to the door to open for the day.

The first of the customers filed in.

"It's a shame you don't remember that guy. Sounds like he was pretty hot." Meg muttered.

"I truly humiliated myself with him. I will not be going to any more company parties with Trina." We filled coffees, handed out pastries and chatted with the regulars.

"Hello." A deep voice came from across the counter.

A shivery spider crawled up my spine. "How can I help you?" My walking wet dream stood in front of me.

He leaned toward me. "How are you feeling?"

I looked around and furrowed my brow. "I'm fine. What can I get for you today?"

He stared at me blankly. "Uh um . . . coffee black with one sugar and a blueberry muffin today."

The hottie paid then moved to the side to wait for his order. He paused before walking away, looked at my scarf, and a sexy grin crossed his face.

"What is that all about?" Meg whispered to me while I got his muffin.

"I have no clue. He's never said more than his order to me." I whispered back.

Meg handed me his coffee and I called his name.

"Thank you," he said with that sexy smirk and his finger rubbed against my hand. What the hell was going on? Was I being punked? Why did that one touch make my panties damp, and the hickey on my neck throb?

He walked away with his coffee and muffin. When he reached the door, Trina walked in. I watched her say hello to him, and they stood for a few minutes and talked. They both looked at me then continued talking.

"What is going on there?" Dean asked.

"No clue. I didn't know Trina knew him."

Trina bid him a farewell and walked toward the counter. "Morning, sunshine." She took one look at my scarf and scoffed. "Has everyone figured out why you are all of a sudden wearing a scarf?"

I blushed.

"We all figured it out rather quickly." Sean bumped shoulders with me.

Trina smiled. "I guess everyone saw the guy who gave it to her too?"

The color drained from my face.

"What?" Everyone said at once.

She furrowed her brow and looked at everyone. "Cierra, you didn't introduce him to everyone?"

I could feel my eyes bug out. "I have no clue who you are talking about. I don't remember the guy. I only remember snippets at best."

Trina looked at me then started laughing. She was laughing so hard she was crying. "Oh my God! You are such a lush."

"Oh, shut it. It's all your fault I drank so much. Those parties are so boring. I was forced to drink my way through it.

"You're a total lush." Dean said. "Who was the guy? I am dying here."

Trina wiped tears from her eyes. "It was the guy I was talking to at the door."

"Fuck!" I dropped the coffee I had in my hand, spilling it all over my apron, pants and counter. I made quick work of wiping up my mess.

"Fuck is right." Dean said looking at me. "How the hell could you miss making out with him? You've ogled him since he started coming in here six months ago."

Shaking my head, I tried desperately to see if Trina was right. "I don't know. He felt familiar. I didn't recognize him."

"This is going to get fun now." Sean said.

"I really can't believe you didn't realize that was him." She turned to Dean, Sean and Meg. "He is the new CEO of WTR Investments, Justin Remington."

"Wait a minute, that can't be right. He gave us his name. It's Jay." I said protesting.

She shrugged. "I don't know why he gave you that name, but I know what his name is and it's Justin Remington."

"It can't be right," I said again.

"Well, he was the one you puked on. He was also the one holding your hair back while you upchucked in the ladies' room."

"Oh dear God!"

"You didn't tell that, muffin. If a man is willing to do that, then he is into you," Dean sighed.

"I don't get drunk like you do, but I know my boyfriend wouldn't do that for me." Meg let out a sigh too.

"Oh my God! You people act like I get drunk all the time." I threw my hands up in frustration. "It was a fluke thing at a stupid Christmas party. It won't happen again." I emphasized by slapping my hand on the counter.

Everyone stared at me slack-jawed.

"Ok, sweetie. I've got to go. I will call you tonight."

"Yeah, ok." I said to Trina's retreating back.

I looked around at my co-workers. "Well, you know what this means now?"

"What?" Sean asked.

"I can never come back to work here."

CHAPTER 5

*A*fter my fiasco at work, tonight was the perfect night to binge-watch on Netflix. Binging on my favorite British documentaries, eating Chinese and finishing off a pint of my favorite ice cream sounded perfect.

Halfway through the documentary on the Tower of London, my phone rang.

"Hello?" I said with a spoonful of ice cream in my mouth.

"Darling!"

Oh, shit! I forgot to look at the caller ID. "Mom?"

"Yes, darling. How are you?" She asked in an aristocratic tone.

"I'm fine. Why are you talking that way?" I asked while taking another scoop of ice cream.

"The playhouse is doing an adaptation of *A Streetcar Named Desire* and I am Blanche."

"Uh mom, why are you talking like an aristocratic British woman?"

"Because we are doing a British adaptation." She said like the explanation was self-explanatory.

"Wait! If the adaptation was by a British person, that doesn't mean the characters change. They are still southern."

"That's part of the adaptation. It's also a musical. I have quite a few solos." OH DEAR LORD! The last time my mom sang, cats came around thinking it was a mating call.

"Oh. Well, that's good." I lied.

"You are going to come see me when it opens right?"

"Uh, well, I am going to have to see what my work schedule looks like."

"Ok, darling. Your father wants to talk to you. Make sure you ask him about the football."

"Will do, mom."

"Love you, Cierra."

"Love you, too." There was a pause, muffled whispers and a loud crinkling sound."

"Hello, sweetie."

"Hi, Dad. How are things going?" I asked pausing my documentary.

"Good. The damn Giants benched our best running back and now our fool kicker is the only offensive weapon we have. So, there goes that season and my fantasy team. So, things suck right now. "

Since my dad retired, he has become obsessed with fantasy sports. He watched ESPN even more now than he did when I was growing up. He has spreadsheets and binders full of stats, pro players, and college players eligible for draft and schedules. He was an accountant until his company outsourced and gave him an ultimatum of retirement or being let go. He chose retirement.

"I'm sorry to hear that dad. I'm sure things will get better by next season."

"Well, there is always my fantasy hockey and basketball leagues and then my college basketball brackets."

"This is true. So, you needed to talk to me."

"Yeah. Hold on a sec." I heard some shuffling, a door opening and closing and then silence. "Are you still there?"

"Yep. I'm here."

"Ok. Good. You are coming to this ridiculous thing your mother is in, aren't you?"

"Uh . . ."

"Oh no you don't. You better make sure your ass is here. Bring those friends of yours, too. If I have to suffer through this for the next few months, you can be here for one night."

"Is it that good?"

"I have invested in earplugs. Your mother caught me with them, and I just told her they are Bluetooth earbuds."

I laughed. "I will see what I can do, dad."

"You better see that your ass is here on opening night. You know what would be helpful?"

"What?"

"If you got a boyfriend by then. Your mother would be more consumed with that than asking us how she was."

"I will see if I can get one by then, but I'm not making promises."

"Hmmm . . . Oh no! I gotta go, Cierra. It's practice time, and I need to use my Bluetooth earbuds. Love you."

"Love you too, dad. Talk to you again soon." Silence sounded on the other end of the line. I shrugged, restarted the movie, and snuggled into the couch.

A banging at the door jerked me from enjoying the last of my ice cream. I groaned and got up from the couch. I checked my reflection in the mirror, I was wearing my favorite leggings with a hole in the knee, an oversized t-shirt with a new chocolate stain and mismatched socks.

When I looked through the peephole, Trina and Dinah stared back.

"I know your ass is looking at us through the peephole. Open the damn door, I have to pee." Dinah yelled.

I sighed. There went my relaxing night. "What do you two want?" I asked when I opened the door.

Dinah pushed her way in and ran/walked to the bathroom.

Trina went straight to the couch and plopped down. "I have news to tell you."

"Ok." I said and waited for her to tell me.

"I can't tell you until Dinah is here."

Rolling my shoulders and cracking my neck, I looked at Trina.

Dinah stormed out of the bathroom. "Feel better?" I asked.

"Definitely." She sat in the chair next to my couch and looked at Trina.

"So, what is it?" I asked.

"I got a promotion today. They are promoting me to senior vice president."

"Holy crap! That is awesome!" I pulled Trina into a hug. My smile felt a bit too tight. Though I was incredibly happy for Trina getting her dream job I was also jealous.

"That's not all though." She paused and looked at me. "The corporate event planner quit yesterday, and they are looking for a new one. I kinda put your name in, and they want to interview you."

Blinking at her, I couldn't process what she just told me. "Event planner?"

"Yeah, like your dream job." Dinah said.

"Wow . . . I don't even know what to say." I said.

"Say you will go to the interview tomorrow at 3 p.m. I checked with Dean and Sean on your schedule."

"You talked to Dean and Sean? They weren't pissed at the idea of me getting another job?"

"Hell no! My brother has always known that you were meant for more." Dinah said.

"Look, it's just an interview, Cierra. Take it one step at a time. If you don't get this, maybe this will encourage you to go for something more than being a barista." Trina squeezed my hand.

Taking a deep breath, I nodded my ok.

"Good." Trina and Dinah said in unison.

"I have one stipulation to the two of you."

They both looked at me speculatively.

"You two are going to come with me to my mom's musical in a couple months." I smiled smugly.

"Oh no!" They groaned.

"Oh yes!"

I told them about my mom's community acting troupe the musical version of *A Streetcar Named Desire* with the British accents. I even told them about my dad's ruse of his earbuds. Each got its own respective groan.

"Last, but not least, my dad asked me to find a boyfriend by then. That way he could distract my mom, and we won't have to lie about her singing."

"Well, it sounds like you have the hardest part." Trina said.

"I may have some of my own earbuds I can use for that night." Dinah smirked.

I shook my head and shooed them out of my apartment with promises of calling tomorrow after the interview.

AT 2:45 p.m. the next day, I stood outside WTR Investments. Before walking into the building, I double-checked my appearance in the windows. In the reflection, I ran my sweaty palms over my skirt, straightened my jacket and took a deep breath. Head held high, I walked in with confidence.

Behind the reception desk sat a young woman. After a phone call, she asked for my name. She gave clipped directions then directed me to the bank of elevators. My heels clicked on the tile floors drawing attention to me. The man standing in front of the elevators turned and looked at me. Breath caught in my chest. Justin Remington was standing there with a confused look on his face.

His cologne wafted around me. Naughty thoughts floated through my head. My shaking hands began to sweat and itch. All I wanted to do was run my hands over his chest again and feel his lips as they skimmed down my neck. As if he could read my thoughts, a sexy lopsided grin took over his face. Just in time the elevator dinged its arrival. I stepped quickly onto the elevator pushing ten. Justin followed. He pushed his floor's button of twelve. He stepped close to me. His arm brushed mine causing me to shiver.

He cleared his throat. "Hello."

I looked anywhere but at him. He was a complication I didn't need right then.

"Figure out how we met yet?" He asked.

I sighed. "Two Beans."

He leaned down close to my ear. "You know I am not referring to the coffee shop."

A chill ran through me. I stood a little straighter and willed the stupid elevator to move faster.

"Why are you here?" He asked.

"Job interview." Sticking to one to two words would be safe.

"The event planner position?"

"Yes."

"Hmm . . ."

I looked at his reflection in the elevator doors. He smirked at me and ran his tongue over his bottom lip.

Dammit! I shouldn't have looked.

Ding!

The elevator opened up to my floor. As I hurried out of the elevator I heard him say, "I'm sure I will see you again soon, Cierra."

I turned and looked at him. His sexy grin was the last thing I saw before the elevator doors shut.

CHAPTER 6

"So, how did the interview go?" Dean asked the next day.

"It went really well. They told me they would let me know soon. I guess they want someone to start training before the new year."

Dean nodded. "They better get on it. The new year is only a few weeks away."

I looked around at the café. Dean and Sean were still decorating for Christmas. Today, they were determined to make gingerbread houses to put on each table as decoration.

"How is your house coming along?" Sean asked walking from the back room with more icing.

"This sucks. You two definitely don't pay me enough to do this." The wall I'd been painstakingly trying to get to stand up, crashed down.

"You are shitty at this." Dinah said. She already had ten done. All looked impressive.

"Thanks, Dinah. Don't you have your own business to go run?" I asked.

"Shut it, Cierra. I need Dinah here. She is making up for your sad little house." Dean said looking back at his gingerbread house.

The door chimed letting me escape the hell of doing the most pointless holiday tradition.

"Go ahead and finish mine." I said to Dinah as I rounded the corner to wait on my customer.

"Finish yours? Burn yours to the ground would be a better option." She said looking at my pile of gingerbread and mess of dried icing.

"Whichever works is fine with me." I replied.

"How can I help—" I spoke too soon about hell.

"Hello, Cierra." Justin Remington said.

I cleared my throat and tried not to blush harder than I already was. "What can I get you?"

Smirking, he just stared at me.

I sighed. "Well?"

"Tell me."

I frowned. "Tell you what?"

"Where do you know me?"

I looked around and saw Dinah, Dean, and Sean watching us like they were watching a telenovela on a Sunday afternoon.

"I don't know what you're—" He cut me off.

"Are you still playing this game?" He glared at me. "I'm done playing this game." He leaned in so that only I could hear him. "I remember how you feel under my hands. I remember how you tasted and how you smelled. You won't get out of my head. I can't fight this anymore."

I looked at him. My mouth was hanging open and when I clicked it shut, I bit my tongue.

Dammit!

Pain shot through me, and I winced.

"I will take a black coffee with one sugar, please." All teasing was gone. His eyes became flat, and his face blanked.

I realized he thought my grimace was about what he said. "I'm thorry. I bit my tongue." Now, I sounded like an idiot.

He just nodded and looked down at his phone.

Meg handed me his coffee and gave me a motion that said to talk to him.

"Here you are, Jay." I went to hand him his coffee. "For what it's worth, I liked your tie." His blue/gray eyes met mine and he pasted that sexy grin on his face. Nodding once more, he took his coffee and left.

I watched him leave and sighed.

"Holy shit! I need to step outside to cool off from that." Dinah fanned herself and walked out.

"She's just going to watch him walk away, isn't she?" I said to Dean.

He smiled and nodded. "So, what did he say to you? It had to be good because your face was priceless."

I smiled and shook my head. "Nothing."

"Ugh! You're a horrible employee," he said.

Before I could come up with a snappy retort my cell phone buzzed. A number I didn't recognize popped up. Hoping it was WTR calling me back, I picked up.

"Hello?"

"I liked your sweater too." A deep voice said.

I blushed and walked to a quiet corner of the café. "How did you get my number?"

He chuckled. "The girl making the coffee wrote it on the cup. So, I have an important question to ask."

"Ok."

"Will you come with me to dinner tonight?" In the background, I could hear traffic passing by. My mind whirled. What do you say when a really hot guy who has seen you puke and make a fool out of yourself asks you out?

"Is something wrong with you?" That wasn't what you say. Damn my lack of filter.

"What?"

"Crap! I didn't mean to say that, but I have no filter sometimes. Sorry." I backtracked.

"No. Tell me why you'd ask that."

I sighed. Damn my mouth. "How could you possibly want to go out with me when I threw up on you, practically molested you on the dance floor and overall made a huge fool out of myself? What the hell is appealing in that?"

He was quiet for a while. So long I'd have thought he'd hung up if I didn't still hear the bustling of people and traffic. "Can I be honest with you?"

"Definitely. I prefer that in my stalkers."

He chuckled again. "I've actually wanted to ask you out for months." I sucked in a breath and choked on my gum. "Oh my God! Are you ok?"

"Yes." I wheezed. "Breathing is new to me. Pardon me while I get the hang of it."

He laughed again. "As I was saying, I've wanted to ask you out for a while now." He paused again. "You didn't choke again did you?"

"No, smart ass. Keep going or I'm hanging up and you'll never know my answer."

"Ok . . . ok. Well, when I saw you at the Christmas party I thought I'd finally get my chance, but you didn't seem to recognize me. Then when we danced, well, I needed a cold shower after."

"So, you are just ignoring the vomiting thing?"

"I'm not gonna lie that was pretty gross, but for some reason I still wanted to be there holding your hair back. I can't explain it." My panties melted just a little.

I gave it a few heartbeats before I finally answered. "Ok, six o'clock outside of the Two Beans."

"I could pick you up at your house."

"Two Beans is fine. I'm still not a hundred percent sure you aren't a crazy stalker."

"Cierra, I am not—"

I cut him off with a laugh. "If you want to be with me, you have got to get better at understanding sarcasm and joking."

He sighed. "I'm usually a really good bullshit detector."

"Yeah. Well, you haven't even begun to experience my bullshit." I grimaced. "Wait I don't think that came out right."

He laughed. "I've got to go, but I will see you tonight. Bye, Cierra."

I smiled. "Bye, Justin."

After hanging up my phone, I stood at the window and looked outside. It was getting colder outside, and people were bustling around with more and more packages. Couples walked by holding hands and cuddling close. My mind was buzzing with the call I just ended but looking out into the world full of holiday spirit, it helped to calm me down.

"Did you just schedule a date?" Dinah asked.

I jumped and turned around. Sean, Dean, and Dinah were standing a foot away with her arms crossed. I had been so consumed with the call I hadn't realized I had an audience.

"Uhm . . . yeah I did."

"Was it with that Sex-on-a-Stick that comes in here every morning?" Dean asked and got a jab in the side by Sean.

"Yeah it is."

"This is huge. I'm glad I've been texting Katrina this whole time. She is in the know and gives you two thumbs up." Dinah showed me her phone where there were two thumbs up emojis.

"I'm going to have to cut my shift short today guys." I said taking my apron off and handing it over to Sean.

"Well, of course, muffin. You need to go home and pamper yourself. Make sure you shave and pluck everywhere." Dean made a motion encompassing my whole body.

"Wow. I love that you guys are supportive but sometimes it's a bit much."

"Don't worry, hun. We will be here waiting when you come back to meet Mr. Sexy." Sean said.

"Oh, great." I said flatly.

"Cierra, you need to get your ass in gear. What are you going to wear? Do you even know where you're going?"

A flood of panic flowed over me. "I have no idea." I said. "But, anything can be better than the ugly sweater and vomit I wore the last time we really hung out."

"That is true. If you go with a sexy LBD and knee boots with your hair pulled back, you will knock him dead." Dinah said nicely.

I smiled. "Sounds like a plan."

I ran to the breakroom and grabbed my jacket and purse.

"We will be here when you come back." Dean said waving me out the door. I ignored him and rushed down the sidewalk. I had a hot date to get ready for.

CHAPTER 7

*A*t six fifteen, I was freezing my ass off in front of Two Beans and a Latte. He was fifteen minutes late, and I was very much regretting my decision of wearing a dress. My blue velvet dress had three-quarter length sleeves and skimmed the tops of my knees. The black three-inch knee-high boots were pinching my toes with each step I took. Though I decided to wear my hair down with the sides pulled up and my long black jacket with a scarf, it still wasn't near enough to keep me warm. If Justin kept me waiting any longer, the anger burning in my blood would be warming me up.

Pacing in front of the Two Beans made me quite the entertaining spectacle for my friends inside. Dinah and Trina sat at a table close to the door. Each time I walked by, Dinah would tap on the window and make an "I will kill him" sign by slashing across her neck. Trina sat wringing her hands trying to calm down Dinah. Dean, Sean, and Meg tried to look like they were decorating but each time I caught them staring at me with a pitying look.

I pulled my phone out of my small clutch. The asshole hadn't texted or called. Why did he bother to ask me out if he was just going to stand me up? I went back to pacing. My mind was going through every possible scenario. What if he got hit by a car? What if he had a stroke? What if his secretary needed him to stay late to work on "reports", which was just her way of seducing him? What if he slipped and fell and got amnesia forgetting all about the date? What if he was just punking me? God help him if the last one was the answer. His balls would be mine.

As I was running through the scenarios and pacing I walked right into a hard body. Strong hands wrapped around my upper arms to steady me from falling. Looking into his gorgeous eyes, I completely forgot about how pissed I was. I forgot about the cold and found myself shivering from his touch. Ugh! I was pathetic.

Pulling quickly out of his arms, my boot heel slipped on a slick spot on the pavement. His hands grabbed me again to save me from my fall. Again. Like I said . . .pathetic.

"I'm so sorry, Cierra. I got caught in traffic."

I stepped out of his arms and crossed mine across my chest. "Are you seriously using the traffic excuse on me?"

"Uhm . . . yes." He shrugged. Then a sly smirk started to spread across his face.

That arrogant smirk made me want to punch his gorgeous face in. "Maybe we should do this another time." I started to walk away, and he grabbed my arm again.

"Wait. I'm sorry, Cierra." He sighed and ran his hand through his hair tousling it perfectly, of course.

Ugh, I hated him.

"Why?"

He licked his lips and looked at me. "I was late because I stopped to get a surprise for you."

I pursed my lips. "What surprise?"

"It's in my car." He waved his hand toward a little sports car idling next to the curb. It was quite the sexy car. Ugh! I hated him even more.

"Are you trying to lure me into your panel van with candy?"

"What are you talking about?"

I shook my head and waved my hand. "Nevermind. The surprise better not be duct tape, rope, and handcuffs."

"If that's the kind of surprise you like," he smirked, "then I will do that next time."

A banging came from the window of the Two Beans. Dinah yelled through the glass, "Don't go into the van for cheap candy! It better be good!"

I rolled my eyes. "The candy better be good."

He smiled. "Come with me. I promise you will like my lollipop."

I snort laughed in the most undignified way and slapped my hand over my mouth. "I won't be licking any lollipops tonight, handsome." I patted him on his chest and walked toward his car.

He opened the door for me. When I looked inside, purple and blue roses sat on the seat with a box of what looked like dark chocolate candy from a high-end candy store. I looked at him, bent to pick up my surprise, and waved them over toward the window.

"Get in the van!" Dinah and Trina shouted.

I moved to get into the car. Justin leaned into the car and asked, "Disappointed they aren't handcuffs?"

Looking up at his too handsome face, I said, "No, because I have my own." I opened my purse and pulled out the pink fuzzy handcuffs, Dinah had given me as a joke. I'd found them earlier when I was searching for gum.

The look on his face was priceless. It was a mixture of intrigue, desire, and shock.

Pulling the door shut, I sat back and buckled up.

The warmth of the heated seats seeped into my body. I sighed at the pure ecstasy that was warmth after being cold. I must have moaned because Justin cleared his throat.

"Uhm . . . ready to go?"

I smirked and turned my head to face him. "Yes, just enjoying being warm." I rubbed my hands on my thighs bringing his attention to the bit of skin he could see where my dress ended, and my boots began.

"Ok," he said and put the car in drive.

I buckled my seat belt as he took off. He wove between cars as if he had no worries about speed limits or traffic laws. I immediately held onto the "Oh Shit" handle when he barely missed lamp post.

He glanced over and smiled. "Scared?"

I gripped the handle tighter as he sped up. "No. I just prefer to live through this date."

He laughed. "I'm a perfectly capable driver."

"Sure."

"Cierra, you are perfectly safe in my car." He said this as he took a turn so tight I swear there were only two tires on the ground.

"I'd feel better if the four tires stayed on the ground, and you were relatively close to the speed limit."

The car squealed into the restaurant's parking lot and up to the valet. Screeching to a hault, the people near the valet jumped back.

Smirking, he looked at me. "See. Safe and sound."

"Yeah, I don't know about that." I reached for the door handle.

"Wait." He said jumped out and ran around to open my door. "My lady." He offered me his hand and helped me out of the warm car.

"Thanks."

Justin linked his hand with mine and led me into The Grande Teatro Torsal. One of the most sought-after reservations in town, it was a former theatre that was transformed into an elegant Italian restaurant. A crystal chandelier hung in the entryway by the hostess stand. Waterfalls, that were definitely not part of the original theatre, flanked either side of the lobby. An intricate mural of angels, gods, and devils still covered the ceiling. Ornate carvings were still prominent throughout the building. The elegance was almost too much.

A young woman holding an iPad and wearing a headset approached. "Mr. Remington, please follow me."

Justin tucked my arm into his, and we followed her. The dining area was more modern. The remnants of the theatre were no longer visible. Tables lined the walls. Fireplaces glowed. Warmth from each fireplace dually worked as heating and light sources. Each table had a small candle lending to a sense of intimacy. It appeared those were the only sources of light.

With such little lighting and my penchance for being clumsy, I nearly fell three times before we were seated. White linen tablecloths adorned each table. Elegantly dressed couples murmured as we passed. I glanced down at my Target purchased outfit and drew my coat closer.

The hostess stopped at a secluded table with a reserved card. She removed the sign placing menus in front of each seat. Justin attempted to remove my coat. His second tug forced me to remove it before I caused a scene. He passed it to the hostess while he pulled out my chair.

Our beautiful surroundings had me in awe. I continued stare like a slack jawed local when Justin finally took his seat. He fit here. I didn't.

"I forgot to tell you this, but you look stunning tonight," he said unfolding his napkin skillfully.

"Thank you. I don't quite fit though." I smiled. "You, on the other hand, could be their poster boy."

"What do you mean you don't fit?"

I scoffed. "Look at the other women around here."

"I don't want to. Do you know why?"

I shrugged.

"The only woman I want to look at is sitting in front of me. She is sexy and quite frankly making my pants quite uncomfortable."

I choked on my water and blushed.

He grinned. "So, am I still Mr. McSexypants?"

"What?" I rasped out.

He started looking at his menu. "That's what you were calling me during the party."

I blushed so hot I thought I was going to set the tablecloth on fire. "I don't remember that," I muttered.

He laughed. "Do you want anything to drink?"

I shrugged. "Wine would be nice. I will let you pick."

"What? No vodka and pineapple?" He smirked.

"Oh my God! Are you going to just keep reminding me about that night?"

"I might. You look pretty sexy when you blush."

I rolled my eyes. "Keep bringing that night up, and you will find yourself eating alone while I Uber it outta here."

He raised his hands in surrender. "Ok. I won't bring it up anymore tonight."

"Tonight?"

"I can't say I will never bring it up again. Especially when it is such a memorable evening for me."

Before I could tell him where to stick his memorable evening the waitress arrived. Justin ordered a red wine that had an unpronounceable name.

We sat quietly looking at the menu until the waitress poured the wine. She took our orders of steak for me and fish for him. Nothing had a price on the items, but I figured I'd at least eat well.

"You surprise me," he said taking a sip of his wine.

"A lot of people say that about me. What did I do?"

"You ordered steak."

"Steak? That surprises you?" I blushed. Well, shit, how much was the steak? Did I just order a thousand dollar steak?

"Most women I take out order a small side salad and a water."

"Oh. Well those women are idiots. I bet when they get home they have a whole meal without you. They didn't want you to see them eat," I shrugged.

"Probably, but I like that you are real like that."

I stared at him and furrowed my brow. "I don't know any other way to be."

"Good. How did your interview go?" He asked.

"I think it went well, but who knows. All I want is to have a grown-up job in the field I studied in college."

"A grown-up job?"

"Yeah. I've worked at Two Beans since I was in high school. Don't get me wrong, I love it there and I love Dean and Sean. They are really the best bosses, but I'd like to get a job where I can use my expensive college education."

"What did you go to college for?"

"Business and event management."

"Hmm. Have you heard back yet?"

"No, but I wouldn't be surprised if I didn't get it."

"Why?"

"I don't have the extensive background others probably have."

"Hmm." He said taking another sip of wine and stared at me with those eyes I couldn't tear my gaze away from. Finally, I forced myself to take gulp of wine and looked at the tablecloth.

"So, you are awfully young to be a CEO. How did you manage that? Inherit it from a wealthy uncle?" The lame joke fell flat.

"That's pretty much how it happened except it was my dad," he shrugged.

Damn my mouth. I felt my jaw drop. "I'm so sorry. I have a bad habit of putting my foot in my mouth."

"It's ok. I had just come from his memorial service to the Christmas party. That was why I didn't have an ugly sweater on. A tacky Christmas tie was all I could do before going."

"Why in the world did you come to that party?"

He shrugged and took a sip of wine. "My dad and I weren't really close when I was growing up. I grew up knowing I was expected to take over WTR. A different career never even crossed my mind. After college, I interned at WTR. My father insisted I learn every aspect of the company," he said. "For a year and a half, I learned everything from janitorial to CEO. Some of the most important lessons I learned weren't as a CEO but as a janitor. My father understood that each employee was important for making a business work. If you separate yourself from even the smallest position in the company, you lose the respect of your employees. The time I spent learning the business helped to heal my relationship with my father. It wasn't perfect, but I understood him better. " He sighed. "I knew my father would not have wanted me to skip the company party. After his ashes were spread, I put on the tie and went to the party."

I linked my fingers with his for support. His warm fingers squeezed.

"I really just wanted to turn around and walk out, but I saw this girl at the bar. She had the worst sweater on. Her filter was clearly broken, and her incredible tolerance for hard liquor was impressive. You could say she drew me to her."

I blushed.

"So, I stayed, and you made one of the toughest days of my life a lot easier." He kissed my hand. "Thank you, Cierra."

"You're welcome."

Our conversation took a decidedly lighter turn for the rest of the evening. We talked about college, hobbies, favorite foods, bucket lists, and any other trivial information we could think of. The wine flowed between us making our lips looser.

When dinner finally arrived, the aroma had my stomach grumbling loudly. Justin laughed so hard the nearest couple looked annoyed. The steak was phenomenal. With each bite, an obscene moan escaped. Scandalized faces watched me, while Justin smiled with a look of desire in his eyes. Dinner ended with a piece of decadent chocolate truffle cake. We shared one piece with two forks. When we finished, Justin reached across the table. He drew his thumb over the corner of my mouth. Justin stuck his thumb in his mouth sucking the chocolate off. Heat rushed through my body. Flames danced in his eyes as he made an obnoxious moaning sound that had me snorting with laughter.

We retrieved our coats from the coat check. Justin helped me into mine then linked our fingers together. His car was idling at the valet stand when we exited. The drive back to the Two Beans was much slower, and he obeyed most of the traffic laws. He held my hand for the entire drive while we sat listening to southern rock on the radio.

Breaking the silence, I said, "I didn't expect this from you."

"What?" He said squeezing my hand.

"Southern rock?"

He laughed. "Oh, this is just some of the more sedate stuff. I love Iron Maiden, Metallica, and Slayer."

My eyes bugged out of my head. "Definitely not what I expected of a high-powered CEO."

"What did you expect?" He asked pulling up outside of the coffee shop.

I swallowed and looked at him. "Classical, opera or instrumental would be what most billionaire CEOs listen to."

He laughed and leaned in toward me. "Sweetheart, you have to realize there is a lot more to me than being just a sexy CEO."

"Oh, I know. You are so modest." I whispered.

"You have no idea." He leaned in and pressed his lips to mine. His soft lips moved slowly making me feel every stroke through my body. His hands took my face and directed the kiss deeper.

Before things could get completely out of hand, I leaned back against my door. Breathing heavily, I looked at him. His face was flushed and his tongue swiped at his lips.

"I need to go." I finally said.

"Cierra . . ."

"It was a really great time. Thank you, Justin." I quickly got out of the car and walked down the sidewalk.

I heard footsteps running behind me. Spinning around, I saw Justin running toward me. When he caught up, he pulled me into his arms and kissed me again. Flush against him, I could feel his heartbeat syncing with mine. Moaning, he snaked his tongue in my mouth. Tasting the chocolate from the cake and mint from the after dinner mint, my knees went weak.

He pulled away. "Go out with me again, please."

My lust filled gaze couldn't process what he was saying. I blinked a few times and registered him staring at me. "Ok."

He smiled. "Saturday?"

I winced. "Actually, Saturday is tough. I need to go Christmas shopping and go to the shelter."

"I will come with you."

My eyebrows went up to my hairline. "Ok. Pick me up here at 7 a.m. We can grab coffee and a kickass muffin then be on our way."

He smiled, leaned in and kissed me lightly on the lips. "Sounds good, sweetheart." He hugged me one more time and walked back to his car.

My short walk back to my apartment wasn't cold at all. In fact, my body was on fire. I'm glad I had just bought batteries for my battery-operated boyfriend or my B.O.B.

CHAPTER 8

"Well, how did it go?" Trina said leaning at the counter of Two Beans.

"I can't talk about this now. I'm working. Shouldn't you be working too?" I asked while helping a customer and handing coffee to another.

"Yeah, but that's the benefit to being a VP now. Flexible work hours." She winked.

I rolled my eyes. "It was nice. We are going out again Saturday."

"Don't you go to the shelter this weekend?"

"Yep. Apparently, he wants to come with me. It should be fun."

Trina took a sip of her coffee and eyed me. "You must like him to be taking him there."

"More like a little test. Let's see how Obie and Artie treat him." Trina snorted coffee on that.

I laughed at my friend's face.

"Not funny. Anyway, have you heard anything from Tammy in HR yet?"

"No," I sighed. "I didn't think I had that bad of an interview."

"They might be behind. Let me check when I get back to the office." Trina started to walk away then leaned back toward me. "Just so you know, there is no interoffice fraternization policy."

"What?"

"I'm just saying you can still date Mr. McSexypants if you get hired. It might be a bit weird at first, but if it's meant to be, then it will be."

"Ok." I said and went back to filling coffee orders.

The rest of the day my mind would drift back to my evening with Justin. The touch of his hand, his lips on mine and his words about the night we met. Dean pointed out on more than one occasion my dreamy smile and my spaced-out look whenever I was daydreaming about Justin. I still felt like a fool with how I acted the night of the party. Maybe our date on Saturday would allow him to see another side of me.

When my shift finished, I walked to the pizza place around the corner and got a small pizza and salad to go. Walking home with my food in my hands, I could feel my phone vibrating in my back pocket. Ignoring it, I continued to my apartment. Walking down the hallway to my apartment, I heard yelling coming from the apartment across from mine.

"Get back here, you little asshole."

"Don't talk back to me. You know you need your drops."

"Ow! I said no biting or I'd get your balls cut off. You don't want that because you enjoy licking them too much."

I cringed at Mrs. Buchanan's door. Tiptoeing to my door, I tried very hard not to make a sound. Unfortunately, Mrs. Buchanan's hearing was better than any twenty-year-olds.

"Cierra? Is that you, dear?"

I slowly turned around. Mrs. Buchanan had curlers in her bluish grey hair, an apron that said "I've got your hot buns right here" over a yellow shirt and a pair of green leggings with pineapples on them. "Hello, Mrs. Buchanan."

"Oh perfect timing dear. I'm having the hardest time getting Asshole to let me give him his eye drops. Could you please come help me? He just loves you."

She was right. Bubbles a.k.a "Asshole" really did love me. In fact, he was always bound and determined to rub on me whenever I was around. Unfortunately, I had a severe allergy to cats. The glint I saw in that cat's eye every time he rubbed himself on me told me he knew he was making me suffer.

"Let me put this in my apartment and I will be over, Mrs. B."

"Ok, dear. We will be waiting. Just come on in." She shuffled back into her apartment.

The smell from the pizza wafted up when I dropped it on the counter. My stomach rumbled. As much as I wanted sit and eat my pizza, I couldn't say no to Mrs. B. I popped two allergy pills and strolled back to her apartment.

Mrs. Buchanan's apartment was the epitome of a little old lady's apartment. Warmth emanated from there. Almost every surface was covered in either doilies or afghans. Amazing smells billowed from her kitchen. Bookcases filled with possibly every harlequin, regency, and erotica romance book ever made lined the walls. Space not taken up by books and book cases had photos of her family. Mrs. B had mentioned only a few times about her family and husband. School pictures of children and grandchildren framed a large flat screen TV. Under the TV was the latest game systems.

I did a double take. Wait . . . What?

"Mrs. B., are you a gamer now?" I asked looking at the gaming situation.

"Oh yes I am, dear. It is fun. I get to play the RPG and war games with my grandkids."

"Well, I am impressed."

She smiled. "Dear, you must know that there is more to a person than just their appearance."

I furrowed my brow at her. "A guy I met said something like that to me, too."

"OH! You met a gentleman. Is he sexy? Will you be able to stop playing with your little friend in your bedroom?" My jaw dropped. She couldn't possibly know about my B.O.B. Could she? "I was getting worried. I never saw any men, and you always hung out with your friend who likes women . . . what's her name? Dina?"

"Wait? What are you talking about? Dinah is not gay. Also, I don't have anything in my bedroom."

"Oh it's ok, dear. I have my own rabbit and bullet. After, I read some of my stories I need a little help, too. But it's not healthy for a pretty young girl like you to not have someone satisfying her needs on the regular. As for your friend, I just figured with that haircut she wasn't interested in a man. Not many men like to date a woman that looks like a better man than they do." She said waving her hand.

"Uh." I didn't even know what to say next. "Where is asshole at?"

"He's hiding, the little prick. I told him I'd take his favorite pastime away if he didn't get his ass in gear and let me put his eye drops in. He's not listening."

"Favorite pastime?" I regretted it the minute it came out of my mouth.

"He licks his balls like it's an Olympic sport. When I get them chopped off, he won't have anything to lick," she huffed.

I sat on her plastic-covered couch and within a few minutes, Asshole was on my lap nuzzling my chest. "Eye drops, Mrs. B."

Mrs. Buchanan shuffled over giving me the eye drops and mumbled something about a shaved ball-less pussy wouldn't give her any more problems. I just ignored her before I would have to go home and bleach my brain.

Asshole was a very pretty cat, though he lived up to his moniker. His beautiful black, grey, and white coat was soft to the touch but every time I had to touch him, my eyes watered. This made giving him his eye drops even more difficult. Holding the cat in a headlock, I could feel his claws digging into my arms and jeans. He yowled and hissed, but I managed to give him his eye drops with only a few war wounds.

"Thank you, Cierra. Do you want to stay for dinner?"

"Oh, no tank oo, Mrs. B. I need to get ome." My now congested sinuses and watery eyes caused me to talk funny.

"Oh," she said sadly. "Maybe another time."

I sighed. She really knew how to pull on the heartstrings. "How about Saturday night?"

She perked up. "Perfect. I will make a roast, and you can help me milk Asshole's anal glands."

I grimaced and nodded. Her roast was totally worth it. "Sounds like the perfect plan, Mrs. B."

SLEEP EVADED ME ALL NIGHT. Between not being able to breath and feeling itchy, sleep didn't come until early in the morning. Coffee at Two Beans was a must for me to be human.

Jenny, the weekend barista, took my order that included my double shot espresso and Justin's regular coffee. Dinah had just dropped off her Saturday batch of pastries that I couldn't resist.

An empty table by the window called my name. Sitting with the two coffees, I thought about the call I missed yesterday. It was the HR manager for WTR Investments. She called to offer me the job. I needed to email them my response this weekend. The job was set to begin on Monday.

I was lost in thought when Justin walked in. My breath escaped me as it did every day I saw him. He wore jeans that fit him just right, a concert tee with an open buttoned flannel and a pair of Nikes. A jacket and skull cap in his hands. Suits made a woman drool looking at him, but dressed casual made her want to throw panties at him.

I waved him over holding up his coffee. A smile lit his face when he saw me. I felt a flush of heat run through me with his heated gaze. His eyes roamed over me like a caress. My skinny jeans, long-sleeved shirt under a shirt that said, "Sarcasm is a way of life", was hardly impressive to a man used to elegance. Thanks to my late night, my unwashed hair was in a ponytail hidden under my baseball cap. When I tried a flirty smile all that came out was a yawn.

"Are you ok?" He said looking at me closer.

"Had bit of a rough night."

"What happened?"

"It was a delightful combination of being a good Samaritan and getting a job offer."

"That doesn't sound bad."

"Its not really bad, but when being a Good Samaritan means your allergies keep you up and the job offer has you so excited your brain doesn't shut off then it makes for a rough sleepless night."

"I'd say sorry, but I don't know if that is even something to say right now."

I shrugged and finished my coffee. I debated on getting another when Justin who seemed to read my mind said, "Want another?"

"I don't know if I should."

"How do you take it?"

I smiled. "Caramel macchiato with almond milk and two sugars."

He nodded and walked over to the line.

I didn't realize I'd been staring so long when Dean interrupted my ogling. "He really is pretty to look at."

Jumping, I looked at him standing next to me with a strand of lights in his hand. "Where are you putting those?"

Dean smirked. "Around the counter. I may finally be done decorating today. As long as I don't end up at Target between now and Christmas. That place is the devil."

I smiled. "For you maybe. Most people have self-control when it comes to Christmas decorations."

"I guess. So what are you and the Sex-on-a-Stick doing today?"

"I'm taking him to the shelter, Christmas shopping and then maybe Mrs. Buchanan's."

Dean laughed. "You're testing him today, aren't you?"

"No, but he said he wanted to spend time with me. It just so happens that some of the most trying things I do in my life are happening today."

Justin was back at the table and handed me the large coffee. "Hey, man! How are you today?"

"I'm good. Just finishing up the decorations." Dean said showing him the string of lights.

"This place looks great. I always appreciate how you go all out for all the holidays." Justin said.

"Thank you. Some people think we go overboard." Dean said gesturing to me.

I stuck my tongue out at him.

Justin's eyes flashed then looked at Dean. "Some very mature people I am guessing."

I huffed. "Alright, if you two are done, I'd like to get my day started."

Dean looked at me with a mischievous glint then turned to Justin. "Good luck, buddy. Just remember what you do with her doesn't change that we have the best coffee and pastries around."

Justin had a confused look on his face. "Uh ok."

"Let's go." I said grabbing Justin's hand and pulling him out of the chair.

Dragging him out into the cold, the rush of arctic air against my enflamed cheeks was just what I needed. Justin and I walked hand and hand for about five blocks without talking. With the caffeine finally coursing through my veins, I felt like the Energizer Bunny with new batteries. Probably shouldn't have had that second coffee.

"Are you going to tell me where we are going?" Justin broke the silence.

"Huh?"

"Did you even remember I was here?" He joked.

"Of course, I did. I don't normally hold hands with random strange men."

He raised one eyebrow that made him look incredibly sexy.

I huffed. "Fine. We are going to an animal shelter. I volunteer every other Saturday."

A look of surprise crossed his face. "Really?"

"Yeah. Why are you surprised?"

"Well, you did say you had an allergic reaction to your neighbor's cat."

"Oh. I can't go into the cat room, but I walk the dogs, clean the lizard, and snake cages and feed the birds."

"Lizards and snakes?" He said with a shiver.

I smirked. "You aren't scared of a couple little ole snakes and lizards, are you?"

He paled but shook his head.

"Good." I smirked.

Justin appeared to get more and more nervous the closer we got. I glanced over but had to stifle a giggle at him nervously biting his nails. He snapped his eyes, giving me a stern look.

"Here we are," I said pointing to the sign above the entrance. The sign said "Ride a Horse, Save a Husky" and in small print it said "Animal Safe House."

"Cute name," he gulped.

"Oh come on." I pulled him into the shelter.

"Son of a bitch!" squawked Murray the cockatiel. Justin jerked to the side.

"Did that bird just cuss at me?"

"Yes, dumbass." Murray squawked again.

I walked over to pet him and feed him a couple sunflower seeds.

"Love you, sweetness," Murray squawked to me.

Justin looked thoroughly offended. He walked over to the bird and held out his hand with a couple sunflower seeds.

"Beat it, deadbeat," he squawked and lunged at Justin.

Justin squealed and jumped back.

"Good Lord. I thought that was a girl out here." A deep voice came from the reception area. Jonas Williams watched with his arms crossed. He was tall, dark skinned and built like a professional linebacker. No one would know that deep down he is a big softy, especially when it comes to his animals.

I was still doubled over laughing. "I know right?" I managed to rasp out between fits of giggles.

Justin grimaced at me. "I don't find this funny at all."

"Listen, man, it really was hilarious," Jonas said.

I took a deep breath and pulled myself together. "Jonas is right," I said. "Justin Remington, I'd like you to meet Jonas Williams. Jonas, this is my friend Justin."

Jonas stuck his hand out for Justin to shake. He looked at it for a minute, sighed and then shook Jonas's hand.

"Nice to meet you, Justin. Are you here to volunteer, too?"

Justin looked at me and shrugged. "I guess I am."

Jonas smiled.

"Ok, then we can start you easy. You can go ahead and go into the cat room. They need their litter changed, water and fed. When you are done, you can help Cierra," he said pointing him to the cat room. "Oh, and watch out for Spike, Simon and Tabby."

"Why?"

Jonas smiled and walked into the bird room.

Justin looked at me. "What is wrong with those cats he named?"

"I have no idea. I can't work in the cat room, remember?" I smiled.

He squinted at me, turned, and walked into the cat room.

I walked over to the bird room and stuck my head in there. "Really? You know those three terrors are going to hone in on him."

Jonas smiled and said, "I'm hoping he will squeal again." Shaking my head, I walked to the kennels.

All who have volunteered at Ride a Horse knew about Spike, Simon, and Tabby. They were three cute bundles of fur. That's how they lured you in. Once they knew they had your attention they turned into the true terrors they were. They were notorious for biting, clawing, gnawing, dumping their food and water the minute you poured it, and escaping. Especially escaping. Those brilliant kittens plotted and planned. They were usually smarter than most of the volunteers.

One volunteer had his wallet and keys stolen by those three. How it even happened, no one knew. That volunteer never came back. Jonas uses it as a hazing of sorts. If you can handle the terrible trio, you can handle any of the other animals.

Coming to the Ride a Horse animal shelter was my happy place. Only coming twice a month was tough. Helping to find these beautiful creatures their forever homes completed me in a way nothing else in my life did. Dinah and Trina had volunteered with me before. Dinah was the only volunteer to walk into the cat room and come out with the three terrors purring and cuddling in her arms. It was the only time I'd ever seen her using baby talk, calling them little darlings. Seeing them as her minions than little darlings was a bit more accurate. They found their evil overlord in Dinah.

Trina, on the other hand has come a bit more than Dinah. She has been the only volunteer not to be hazed by those terrors. Jonas has a soft spot for her. If I didn't know any better, I'd think he had a crush on her. She found comfort with the animals as well.

While feeding the dogs, the kennel door burst open. Justin stood there looking like he'd been through a tornado. Scratches marred his pretty face, his t-shirt was ripped and he had a limp now.

"Oh my God! What happened?"

"The three little devils happened. I was feeding them and cleaning the litter boxes when a paw reached out and tapped my shoulder. I looked up into three of the cutest kittens I'd ever seen. They were meowing innocently." He shook his head and started pacing. I knew where his story was going.

"Ok. That sounds good." I smiled encouraging him to keep going.

"So, I decided to take them out and play with them for a few minutes. The minute I opened the cage door all three flew at me. One scratched, one bit, and the other some how got my keys and ran under a rack. I tried getting the first two off of me but they just dug in further. So with the two hellions hanging on I walked over to the rack. What I didn't realize was that when they jumped me, I dropped the food I was holding. When I went to walk over to the rack, my feel slipped out from under me and I fell. I think I may have twisted my ankle weird."

The scene flashed in my mind. My mind played a cartoon version. To hide my laughter, I bit the inside of my cheek so hard I tasted blood.

"I finally managed to get up and get those three in their cage, feed them and change the litter. The rest of the cats were fantastic compared to those three. I know why they aren't adopted." He shook his head and sat in the chair by the door.

"Sit there and rest. I'm sorry that was so rough."

He shrugged. "It's ok. Can I help you?"

I shook my head. "Nope. They are almost all fed and then while they eat, I will go clean the lizard cages."

A grimace twisted his face.

"You can help me after that if your leg is ok."

"I'll be fine. Just tell me what you need." He smiled his sexy smirk.

"We will need to walk the dogs so they can do their business. But, let's let them eat first. You can sit in the welcome area while I clean the lizard cages."

Justin and I walked toward the iguana lounge. Jonas tries to come up with fun names for the rooms. Emphasis on the tries. While I am cleaning the few lizard cages, Justin chatted with me. We talked about his job, what he likes to do on his weekends. Surprisingly enough, jet setting on his golden yacht wasn't his top answers. We had a lot of similar interests. He plays hockey in a league during the winter, coaches kids' basketball, and plays a summer slow pitch softball league with all of his father's friends. In between him telling me about himself more, Murray would interject the random "bastard," asshole," "monkey butt lover" and "skiddle me rinky dink". With his last comment, I poked my head out. Justin was standing eye to beak with Murray.

"What the fuck did you just say, Murray?" He asked quietly.

Murray cocked his head and said, "Twigs and berries!"

Justin shook his head and noticed me looking at their interaction. Before he could say anything, I said, "Arguing with Murray never works. Well, it works if you're aiming for people to think you are insane." I giggled like an insane person.

"You are not funny," he huffed and crossed his arms. Getting up with just a little limp, he walked over to me. "Are you done with those things yet?"

I laughed as I put Ghecko the chameleon back into his terrarium.

"They are quite lovely. Especially, Ghecko here." To ease Justin's anxiety toward the lizard, I tapped the glass to get his attention. Ghecko chose that time to hiss and attack the glass. Surprise had me jumping away from the terrarium. Strong arms wrapped around my waist.

"I've got you," he breathed into my ear.

I looked down at his arms hooked around me. Who knew forearms could be so sexy? Also, was that a little color poking out?

Taking his forearm in my hand, I pushed up his sleeve. He had a tattoo. A pretty damn intricate tattoo filled with flowers, knives, spiked hearts and smiling skulls.

"Whoa!" I said oh so articulately.

"What?" He said putting his chin on my shoulder and looking at what I was looking at.

"You have a tattoo. One hell of a tattoo."

I felt him smile against my shoulder. "That isn't my only one. Maybe I can show them all to you sometime."

How the hell did the room get so hot all of a sudden? I felt like one of those southern damsels that need a fan before they swooned.

"Maybe someday." I croaked out.

"Are you two actually going to help today or just make out in the lizard lounge?" Jonas' strong arms bulged as they crossed his chest.

I blushed, pulled out of Justin's arms, scooched by Jonas, and walked back to the kennels.

CHAPTER 9

"What the bloody hell?" Justin exclaimed when Obie jumped into his lap.

I laughed. "That's Obidon. He likes cuddles."

Obidon was a mastiff/shephard/Irish wolfhound mix. Obie was huge but also undeniably one of the best dogs. The only reason Obie hadn't been adopted was because he wouldn't leave his brother. His "brother" Artie was a disabled dachshund that had his back end in specialized wheelchair. While Obie jumped on Justin's lap making him fall into the chair behind him, Artie proceeded to go to town on his leg.

"What the hell is happening right now?" Justin yelled.

"You are getting the Obie and Artie welcome." I laughed.

I grabbed the leashes and whistled. Artie pumped two more times got back down on all fours, looked up at Justin, nodded, huffed, and walked over to me. Obie was ignoring me while Justin petted him absently.

"Obie! Let's go!" I said sternly.

He gave me a solemn look then slowly slid off of Justin and meandered over to me.

Justin let out a breath. "Can I help?"

I nodded. "Grab two leashes and get the dogs in three and four.

They won't have any problems walking with these two troublemakers."

Justin leashed the other two dogs. Obie and Artie led the way through the door. The door opened to a back alley that we took to the sidewalk.

The four dogs walked nicely enjoying their time out of their kennels. Justin had no problems with Hanz and Franz, two terrier mixes. Obie and Artie pulled their normal shenanigans with me but with the added bonus of Obie looking longingly at Justin. I knew how he felt.

It wasn't fair. Even walking dogs, Justin looked like a God who had just stepped off Mt. Olympus.

"Why are you staring at me?" He interrupted my ogling.

I cleared my throat and looked away. "Thought I saw a bug on you."

"You are a shitty liar." He smiled.

"Yeah, well you are a shitty volunteer." An irrational anger started to flow through me.

"I think I'm doing well for my first time. I've never had to do something like this before."

"You've never volunteered before?"

"My parents didn't believe in volunteering. They were philanthropic by donating money."

"You've never really gotten your hands dirty before have you?"

"I've never had to," he shrugged a shoulder. "Doing things like this has always been beneath me."

Red flashed through my vision. "Beneath you?"

"What?" He said keeping in step with me.

I seethed as I walked/dragged Obie and Artie back to the shelter. "Volunteering is beneath you? Actually working for a living is beneath you? You realize that not everyone has been given what you have. That helping people or animals survive isn't beneath anyone. It really says something about a man who holds that view."

He squinted at me. "What is that supposed to mean?"

"It means I have finally seen the real Justin Remington. The Justin Remington that believes in money above everything else. I don't fit with that guy. Money pays my bills but it doesn't run my life. This won't work." I stopped and looked at him.

He looked like I had just slapped him. "What are you talking about? I don't think any of this is beneath me or that because I have money I'm better than you or anyone else." He took a breath. "You're one of those women, aren't you?"

"What women?"

"Women who distrust everyone. Always waiting for the other shoe to drop. So, before it can fall apart, you pick things apart. What is this argument really about? My money? I can't do anything about that. Just because I have money doesn't mean it defines me. You don't know me enough to judge me. Was I brought up to believe getting my hands dirty was "beneath" me? Yes. I was. Do I believe that now?" He took a deep breath. "You are going to have to ask that question. But if you want to keep picking this fight and make assumptions, go right ahead. I can take it."

"Are you fucking kidding me right now?"

"No. What else do you have to tear apart and argue about? Come on, I'm ready."

I shook my head and walked back to the door.

"You aren't going back in until we settle this. Now come on."

An irrational anger flowed through me. He had pointed out exactly what I was doing. That made me even angrier.

I turned back around and saw him in the same place with the same exasperated look on his face. "Money is always going to be an issue. You have it. Your views are around it. It's important to your family. Our lives don't mix." I raised my hands using air quotes for the last portion.

A confused look crossed his face. "What?"

"You know what, Justin? Never mind. There isn't more to say."

He continued to stand there staring at me.

I threw my hands in the air in frustration and attempted to drag Artie and Obie with me. Before taking two steps, I felt a hand on my arm and was spun around.

"What are you-" I was stopped with the press of his lips on mine. I moaned into his mouth and melted into his arms. After a few scorching kisses, I pulled back and looked into his hypnotizing eyes.

"I needed to shut you up. I'm sorry I came across that way. I didn't mean it. I've actually had a great day today and believe me when I say my mom is going to love this story."

I smiled at that and the thought of his mother learning about us gave me butterflies.

"Are we ok now? I believe we have a few more dogs to walk before we can get some lunch."

I nodded because apparently he kissed all the words out of me.

The next hour flew by. We walked the rest of the dogs and even had a chance to play with Obie and Artie. Justin warmed up to them. He threw a ball for little Artie to fetch and continued to pet a now-snoring Obidon.

I walked out to the deserted waiting area and went toward the door to Jonas's office. Reaching up to knock, I heard him raise his voice.

"We had an agreement! You said I had until the new year." Jonas exclaimed.

A tinny voice came out of the speakerphone. "I know what was said Jonas. Unfortunately, I took a look at the budget and I really can't see how you will be able to raise the money. You need to start making decisions about what you are going to do after you shut down."

My blood turned cold. Shut down?

"You are giving me a little under a month to come up with half a million dollars or you're just throwing me and the animals out?"

"Honestly, Jonas, I don't give a damn about those mangy animals. Clearly, they are defective if no one is willing to adopt them. Either get the money or you will find yourself locked out of your precious money pit."

"You are such an asshole."

A laugh came from the phone. "Maybe, but I am the asshole that has the deed to your shelter. Get it done, Jonas. Don't let a few misfits destroy you."

"Goodbye, Cameron."

"Goodbye, Jonas."

Jonas punched his fist on the phone to shut it off. A loud crack sounded, and Jonas collapsed into the chair behind his desk.

"You're going to have to close?" I said.

Jonas jumped and looked up at me. "It would seem."

"We have to do something. We can't just let the bank take the shelter."

Jonas shrugged. "There is nothing I can do. My major donors backed out this year. So, the money I was counting on is not there. Unless you know a charitable billionaire, then it looks like Ride a Horse may not be around come January first."

I did know a billionaire. In fact, he was in the kennels right now.

"I have an idea."

"Well, lay it on me."

"A charity ball."

Jonas furrowed his brow. "I don't know, Cierra. It's a nice idea, but we would have to get this together by January 1st."

"It's totally doable. I just got hired on as a corporate event planner. Plus, I have some connections you don't know about."

Jonas sat silently looking at her. "You really think this could be pulled off?"

"Absolutely." Justin and I said at the same time.

Jonas and I looked at Justin standing behind me in the doorway. "It is definitely something we can do. Let's sit down and sketch out what you'd like this to look like."

Justin sat down in a chair across from Jonas. I pulled out my phone and started to take electronic notes. Venues, extravagance, which animals to bring, theme, food and anything else we could think about I noted. This could really be one of the best parties I have ever planned. As we wrapped up our plan, I looked at Justin and saw him in a whole different light. Trina was right. He was a good guy.

"Earth to Cierra." Jonas said waving a hand in front of my face.

I blinked and looked at the two men smirking at me. "What?"

"Justin asked you if we needed to talk about anything else."

Shaking my head, I shut off my phone and started making mental lists.

We all stood to leave. Reaching his hand out, Justin shook Jonas' hand.

Jonas held fast to his hand. "Don't take this the wrong way but why are you interested in helping? I get why Cierra wants to because she is an institution here. This is just your first time coming here."

Justin smiled. "I'm a good businessman. I can see potential. If I didn't think that this would be a good risk, I wouldn't be helping."

Jonas nodded his head and took it for what it was.

"We better get going." I said to Justin. To Jonas, I said, "I will be in touch later this week about everything that needs to get done."

I walked around the desk and gave Jonas a quick hug. Jonas smiled and gave me another quick squeeze while staring behind me at Justin.

Justin had his hands crossed over his chest glaring at the two of us.

I giggled and then walked over to Justin pulling him with me.

CHAPTER 10

$\mathcal{W}$e walked back toward the café. Thoughts of losing the shelter floated through my head. To ease my mind, Justin discussed everything we needed to do. As we talked our hands linked. It felt so natural it was scary. My emotions were on a never-ending roller coaster. He pulled me to a stop outside of Two Beans.

"Would you have dinner with me tonight?" He asked.

I smiled. "I'd love to, but I already committed to dinner with someone else tonight." Justin visibly deflated. I smiled again. "However, you can come with me. I promised my elderly neighbor that I'd come over and let her feed me. She always makes too much, and she'd love having a handsome guy like you come by."

He smirked. "Sure. I can charm a nice old lady."

I bit my lip holding back my laugh. He had no idea what was coming.

"Oh hello, dear." Mrs. Buchanan said. She must have just been playing video games with her grandchildren because she still had her headset on her head.

"Hello, Mrs. Buchanan."

"Come in. I just finished up with the roast and am working on the potatoes." She said motioning toward the kitchen. "Who is this handsome young man?" She asked looking past me and right at Justin.

"My name is Justin Remington. It's a pleasure to meet you, Mrs. Buchanan." He stuck his hand out for her to shake.

Mrs. B shook her head and grabbed him into a hug. Justin stiffened and jerked.

"Oh. He has a nice firm behind on him, Cierra. You want to keep him."

I blinked at her then looked at Justin. He was standing there blushing.

"Come in, dears." She walked be toward the kitchen.

"What just happened?" I asked.

"Your nice elderly neighbor just pinched my ass."

I laughed. "What?"

"When she went in to hug me, her hand went right to my ass and grabbed." He shook his head and rubbed his ass. "It kinda hurt actually."

I pressed my lips together trying hard not to laugh. I failed miserably.

Justin looked around the apartment and smiled. Mrs. Buchanan stuck her head of the kitchen.

"Have a seat and make yourself at home. Cierra, will you come in here and help me?"

I nodded and looked at Justin. "Will you be ok in here by yourself?"

Before Justin could answer we heard a crash and Mrs. Buchanan said, "Watch it, Asshole."

Justin's eyes got big. "Is someone in there with her?"

I huffed out a laugh. "No. Asshole is her cat." Just when I said that a furry blur shot out of the kitchen and flew in the air. Asshole/Bubbles landed claws out right in Justin's lap.

"Oh shit!" He yelled. Asshole hissed at him and dug in his claws.

I tried prying the cat off his lap but he just dug in harder. "Let go!"

Justin was gritting his teeth and managed to unhook his claws from his jeans. Asshole huffed his disapproval then plopped down next to Justin acting as if he didn't just try to castrate him.

"Are you ok?" I asked.

"I think. Now I understand why his name is Asshole."

"You have no idea. I will be right back. Let me see what Mrs. B needs help with."

Leaving Justin on the plastic covered couch, I walked into the kitchen where Mrs. Buchanan was now stirring gravy on the stove. Her kitchen was neatly organized. The delicious aroma of the roast, potatoes, vegetables and gravy had me drooling. In the corner, food and water dishes for Asshole were tipped over. Clearly that was the racket we'd heard just a few minutes ago.

"What did you need help with Mrs. B?"

"Come over here Cierra." I walked over and stood next to her. "I don't need any help. I wanted to gossip about that juicy piece of man-candy out there."

I snorted a laugh. "Ok."

"So, give an old lady the details. How is he in the sack? I bet he is hung like a horse. He reminds me of my Edward. Oh, the stories I could tell you. He was quite adventurous. I bet Justin is too. What kind of kinks does he have? Does he have one of those secret rooms where you have to sign an agreement with your hard and soft limits?"

Mrs. B read way too much romance. Any other excuse for her questions made me want to stick my head in the oven.

"Um. I can't tell you any of that because we haven't done anything more than kiss."

Mrs. Buchanan stared at me with her mouth hanging open. "Are you joking right now? As long as it's been for you and the amount of batteries you go through, why aren't you climbing that man like a tree? If I were a few years younger, ooo boy I'd show him a thing or two. What is the hold up, Cierra?"

"Uh . . ."

"Do you need my help? I can have a chat with him if you'd like."

"Good Lord, NO!" Mrs. Buchanan startled with my loud tone.

"I was just offering, dear. So, what is the hold up?"

"We aren't in a hurry, Mrs. B. We have plenty of time. We are getting to know each other. I promise I will share the details whenever it happens." My fingers crossed behind my back.

She squinted at me. "You won't tell me, but I will get it out of you when it happens. I'm just happy you finally found someone, sweetie. He looks like a good one." She squeezed my arm and moved past me.

"Do you want me to take any of this out to the table for you?" I asked hoping for a change of subject.

"Sure, dear." She smirked and continued to put the finishing touches on dinner.

Setting the dishes on the table, I looked into the living room area. Justin had tamed the wild heathen cat and was whispering to it while he petted him. The smile I felt on my face was involuntary. This man was weaseling his way into my heart a little by little.

During dinner Mrs. Buchanan was her normal feisty self. She grilled Justin on his feelings and intentions toward me. She gave him pointers on sexual positions that were best for different surfaces according to her and "her Edward's" experience. She talked about my need for batteries every other week. Mrs. Buchanan also talked about her love for her children and grandchildren, her bingo, knitting ladies, and Asshole even when she threatened yet again to have his balls cut off for trying to jump on the dining table.

Justin took everything in stride. His shades of red fluctuated from bright to light pink. When Mrs. B. brought up my battery situation, he looked at me with a smirk and quirked his eyebrow. Blushing, I looked away. I attempted to stop her tirade on how I needed to get laid, but she just ignored me.

We insisted on helping Mrs. Buchanan clean up. When we finished, Mrs. B. batted her eyes at Justin.

"So, Justin dear, would you help me with something?" Mrs. B. said in her best elderly lady voice.

"Of course, Mrs. Buchanan. What do you need?"

"Well, it's something with the cat. I'd ask Cierra to do it, but I know she is terribly allergic." I smirked at him when he looked at me. The squint he gave me told me that he knew something was coming his way.

"I can do it for you. I don't want to see Cierra get sick." Mischief sparked in his eyes.

"Oh, thank you, dear. Can you massage Asshole's anal glands? He has terrible constipation and is rubbing his hole all over my carpet."

Justin looked at her as if she were joking. When he realized she was serious, he looked horrified. "What?"

"You need to massage his anal glands. It helps with his tummy issues." I said helpfully.

"If you sit on the couch when you do it, he should be a good boy." She said carrying Asshole like a baby.

Justin stood from the dinner table and walked slowly over to the couch. He kept glancing at me for reassurance that this was a real thing he was about to do.

After Mrs. Buchanan dropped Asshole in his lap, she walked away with a wink in my direction. Justin struggled with the yowling cat. In that moment, while massage an angry cat's anal glands, he still looked panty-melting hot.

Life wasn't fair.

"Son of a bitch!" Justin yelled.

"Oh stop being a baby." I said continuing to clean the cuts on his arms.

"Let me cut you and then pour the acid in your hand on your arm and see if you like it," he pulled away and covered his arm.

"Oh for crissakes, Justin. I've had these scratches before. If you don't clean them, you can get an infection." I gently pulled his arm back toward me.

He humphed and pouted.

I couldn't help but smile. "I will be gentle. I promise."

He sighed. "Fine. Just do it already."

I lifted my eyebrow at him then gently cleaned his cuts from Asshole's claws. Asshole did not take having his anal glands massaged as something he wanted done to him. Justin ended up with bites and scratches all over his hands and forearms. The bonus for this happening to him was I got a better glimpse at his tattoos.

After cleaning his wounds, I meticulously put ointment on them so they wouldn't get infected. None of the cuts or bites were deep enough to need stitches, but I took my time and looked closely at all of injuries. The muscles in his forearms tensed and rolled each time I had to touch him. I didn't think it was possible to get aroused by forearms, but my damp panties told me that was definitely a thing.

Justin cleared his throat. "Um, Cierra, I think you've taken care of all the wounds. You're just petting me now."

I had been so lost in his muscles and tattoos that I was actually petting him. Shocked out of my dream world, I jolted and dropped the ointment on my carpet. "Dammit."

"I'll get it for you." He picked it up, put the lid back on and handed it to me.

"Thanks." I mumbled. Jumping up a bit too eagerly, I tripped over my carpet and landed on my face while trying to make my way back to the bathroom.

Justin ran over to help me up. "Are you ok? Let me help you up." He tried helping me up, but I refused.

"Just let me lay here and die of embarrassment."

He chuckled then forced me into a sitting position. "Let's take a look." Justin stared at my face, running his hands over my face and neck. He drew his thumb across my lip and gave me a sexy smirk. "Am I ok?" I asked.

"I think you'll live. But you have something right here." He leaned in and softly kissed my lips. I melted toward him and fisted his shirt in my hands. Justin sat back on his butt and crossed his legs. Pulling me into his lap, he forced me to straddle his lap.

Smiling he captured my lips again. His hands slid up my ribcage and across my back, pulling me closer. The ridge of his cock pressed against my core. Our jean clad legs were the only things keeping us separated. As he pulled me closer, I ran my hands up his arms, over his broad shoulders to run my fingers through the hair at the nape of his neck. His muscles rippled under my hands. I tugged his hair to bring his mouth to mine. The savage kiss drew a groan of ecstasy from him. Our tongues tangled. He tasted of mint and soda.

With every groan, my hips ground on his rigid length. His hand slid to my ass pulling me harder against him. Breaking the kiss, I drew in a ragged breath. He kissed down my neck and sucked on my collarbone. Apparently, that was one of my erogenous zones. Tingles shot through me when he bit lightly. My panties were soaked and I desperately wanted relief.

"Oh, Justin." I sighed.

He smiled against the top of the breast he was kissing. Pulling back he looked at me and caressed my face. A look I couldn't identify passed across his face. Leaning in, he kissed my lips so gently and reverently, I could feel every emotion he was feeling with that one kiss. With my lips, I urged him to take it deeper. To give me more. He pulled back and leaned his forehead against mine.

"We need to stop, Cierra," he said in a gruff voice.

"Uh . . . what?"

"We need to stop. Before you get upset, it isn't because I don't want you. Clearly, I do." He gestured to his cock straining against his jeans. "I want us to do this right. I want to go slow with you. You deserve to be cherished, worshipped, and given the world." He leaned in and kissed my forehead.

"So, you don't want to fool around?" I asked after he moved me off his lap.

He moved to grab his jacket and turned to me. "Oh, I definitely want to do that and more with you, sweetheart. Unfortunately, my mother brought me up to treat a lady with respect. Even if my cock is screaming to be inside you right now."

I moaned and slumped on the floor.

"Don't worry, baby. When we finally consummate what we have, you won't be needing those batteries for quite a while."

Groaning, I covered my face. "You won't ever let me live that down, will you?"

My hands were pulled from my face and Justin was squatting next to my prone body. "Don't worry, I have lots of ideas where we can use those toys. However, you won't be needing them because you're lonely." He kissed me slowly one last time.

"Ok." I said dreamily.

Justin chuckled. "See you Monday, sweetheart."

I nodded and looked up at the ceiling. Justin left and shut the door quietly behind him. It still felt like my body was on fire from our short makeout session.

As I was replaying it in my head planning on definitely using my B.O.B. I sat up suddenly and said, "Dammit! I still didn't get to see all those tattoos." Groaning, I lay back done on the floor and closed my eyes with memories of the sexy, complex man who had just left me in such a state that I would need to wring out my panties.

CHAPTER 11

*I*t's been almost a week since my date with Justin. Though it was a very memorable one, I haven't had the chance to think about it too much. Starting my new position at WTR has sent my world spinning.

My trainer's name is Sally and she is the current corporate event planner. Starting first thing Monday morning she has had me cramming more information than my brain could hold. Every night I've come home feeling hung over with information overload.

Today, she has given me the sole task of planning one of the company's smaller upcoming events. It's a fairly simple joint meeting with three different departments. Coordinating schedules, catering, materials and venue has kept me running around like a chicken with its head cut off. I was so deep in my work that I didn't hear the knock on my door. It was the second louder knock that had me glancing up.

"Can I help you?" I asked the man holding flowers in my doorway.

"Are you Cierra Jameson?" He asked looking at the card in his hand.

"That's me."

He nodded then placed the flower arrangement on my desk and

walked away. I opened the card attached and had to sit because my legs no longer held my weight.

Hi Beautiful!

Looks like you are having a great first week. Can't wait to see you again.

Netflix and Dinner, My place, tonight at 7?

Please say yes.

Yours, Justin

P.S I miss your kiss.

"Ooo . . . who are those from?" The high-pitched voice jolted me out of the puddle Justin turned me into.

"Uhm. No one you'd know." I said to Janice Payton, my trainer's assistant.

"Uh huh. Well, whoever it is they certainly like you a lot. There are at least three dozen roses of different colors in here. He must be rich too," she smirked.

I just nodded and held the folded note in my hand.

"Was there anything you needed, Janice?"

She pulled herself away from smelling the roses and looked at me. "Oh, yes. Ms. Roy would like a word, if you aren't too busy."

"Of course. Please send her in."

Janice scurried out of my office, and Trina walked in with a notepad and smirk on her face.

"How can I help you today, Ms. Roy?" I pressed my lips back suppressing a laugh.

"Cut the shit," she said shaking her head and plopping into one of my chairs.

"Sorry, couldn't help it. What's up?"

She eyed the flowers on my desk and moved them to the side. It was an awfully large arrangement.

"Who are those from?" She grinned.

Getting up, I walked over to my door and closed it. "Justin."

"I thought so. Things are going well then?"

"Yes. I think I'm really getting the hang of things around here."

"You know that wasn't what I was talking about."

"I know. I was trying to avoid the topic."

She just stared at me.

Sighing, I said, "It appears things are going well there, too."

"Good."

Furrowing my brow, I looked at her. "Was there a reason you came down here?"

"Oh. I was down the hall when I saw the flower delivery. I was going to stop by anyway, but the flowers gave me a reason."

I rolled my eyes. Before I could answer her, my phone rang. She got up to leave and gave me a little wave as I picked up the phone.

"Hello? This is Cierra Jameson."

"Did you like the flowers?" The deep voice shot right to my core, causing goosebumps to rise along my arms.

Clearing my throat, I answered, "Yes, sir. They are very nice."

"Ooo I like you calling me *sir*."

I choked.

He laughed his deep, seductive laugh. "So, are we on for tonight?"

I looked down at the note that was attached to the flowers. "Is this business or personal?" I whispered so Janice couldn't overhear my conversation.

"Oh Ms. Jameson, my business with you is entirely personal."

I smiled. "The answer is yes then."

"Good. I have to leave the office early today for a meeting across town, but I will have my car waiting for you at 5 p.m. out front."

"Ok."

I could hear the smile in his voice when he said, "See you tonight, beautiful."

Sighing, I hung up the phone and slumped back in my chair.

CHAPTER 12

"*S*ee you tomorrow, Cierra," Janice said from her desk.

Waving, I made my way over to the elevator. The butterflies in my stomach started working overtime, and my palms became sweaty. I didn't understand why I was so nervous.

"Getting in, Cierra?"

I jolted from my thoughts and saw Trina holding the elevator door open for me.

"Yep. Just doing a mental list of things I need to do."

"Uh huh. Need a ride home tonight?"

I cleared my throat. "Not tonight. Thanks for the offer though."

"Going to his place tonight?" she smiled, watching the numbers go down with the elevator.

"Yep."

She smiled again.

The elevator finally landed, and we walked together across the lobby. A man in a chauffeur's uniform stood to the side with his hat in his hand.

"That's your ride." Trina nudged me toward the man.

The chauffeur stood straight as I was walking toward him.

"Ms. Jameson?" he asked.

"Yes."

"Mr. Remington asked that I drive you. Please follow me." He walked briskly outside. A tinted sedan was idling at the curb. He opened the door for me to get in.

"Thank you," I said. He tipped his hat and jogged around to the driver's side.

The sedan was luxurious. I thought the car that Justin picked me up in the previous date was fancy, but this one was elegant. Running my hands over the soft leather seats, it felt like I was riding in a dream. I leaned back and watched the city go by. The warmth and softness was so inviting I felt myself falling asleep. Before I could fall asleep, I jolted myself upright.

"You can sleep, Miss. We have a bit of a drive. I will wake you when we get close."

"Are you sure?" I yawned.

"Yes, Miss."

"Ok. Thank you . . . wait, what is your name?"

"Sam."

"Ok. Thank you, Sam." I only intended to close my eyes for a minute.

My dream world was so warm and soft. Justin held me in his arms, murmuring the sweetest words. I snuggled closer. His strong tattooed arms hugged me around my middle, pulling me against his achingly hard cock. I moaned when I felt his kiss on my neck. He was dragging his tongue down my neck. It felt too good to be real. He nuzzled my neck and then licked my cheek. Wait . . . what? He licked my cheek again and barked.

I jolted upright and saw a furry muzzle in front of my face. Its tongue licked me again on my face. A beautiful golden retriever was sitting next to me. Looking around, I was confused. A gray and blue blanket was pooled around my waist. I was sitting on a grey suede sofa. It was soft under my hands. There was a giant TV on the wall and a glass coffee table behind the dog. Gorgeous black and white landscape pictures hung throughout the room. There were also a few framed family pictures interspersed. The most fantastic thing about the room were the multiple mahogany bookcases lined along the wall.

They were filled to the brim with books. My inner bookworm called out to look at them. But, first I needed to figure out where in the hell I was.

Blinking, I tried to remember where I was at and how I got here. The last thing I remembered was that elegant sedan. I must have fallen asleep but that doesn't explain why I was clearly napping on this couch. The fur face in front of me started to nudge my hand. I petted the dog aimlessly. Music came from down the hall. A sweet baritone voice sang along. Standing, I folded the blanket and left it neatly on the couch.

On bare feet, I tip-toed down the hallway to see if I knew the singer. The dog jogged down the hall in front of me. The hallway was darkened except for the light coming from the room at the end. Walking toward the light, I entered into the kitchen. Not just any kitchen though. This huge space would make even Gordon Ramsey swoon.

The kitchen was illuminated with warm light. It had beautiful, dark mahogany cabinets with grey, white, and red granite countertops. The island had a huge farm sink. Two industrial stoves were filled with pots cooking different items. The smell alone would have drawn me here if it hadn't been for the singing. The stainless steel refrigerator matched the dishwasher and stoves perfectly. In and among this beautiful kitchen was Justin.

He wore low slung jeans, a grey t-shirt, and a backwards ball cap, hiding his dirty blonde hair. He was singing along to the music filtering out from hidden speakers. His voice, like everything else about him, was perfect. That being said, his dancing skills were lacking. He definitely wasn't a stripper in another lifetime. He had the bump and grind down but that was about it. I tried to recall our time dancing during that Christmas party, but I was too drunk to remember if he was good or not.

Using the ladle as a microphone, he danced around in front of the stoves. Stirring and adding spices like a pro made him even hotter. How was that even possible with the dance moves he had? He spun around with the grace of one of the ballerina hippos from *Fantasia*. When he saw me standing there gawking he screeched to a halt, dropping the ladle. The furry beast ran over snatched the utensil off of the ground and ran away with it.

"Rascal! Get back here!" He said running after the dog.

A few minutes later, Justin sauntered back into the kitchen.

"Have a nice nap, sleepyhead?" he asked. Throwing the ladle into the sink, he retrieved another spoon to use for his stirring.

"Uh, yeah. I have a couple questions."

He stirred one of the pots and then stood leaning against counter. Crossing his arms across his chest, Justin forced me to look at the rippling muscles he was flexing. "Go ahead, sweetheart," he smirked.

"How did I end up on your couch? How long have I been asleep? Where are my shoes, purse, and laptop bag? What smells so good because I am starving and could probably eat a horse."

He held up one finger. "First, I carried you from the car to my couch."

Holding up a second finger. "Second, you have only been here for forty-five minutes. So, I'd say you've been sleeping for about an hour and a half."

Adding a third finger. "All of your belongings are in the closet down the hall."

Flashing four fingers now. "I am making homemade pasta and sauce with fresh bread in the oven." He glanced over at the clock on the stove. "It should be ready in about ten minutes."

I stood gaping at him. "You carried me from the car to the couch? Why? Why didn't Sam just wake me up when we got here?"

"He tried. You were slumped against the window drooling."

"I was not."

"You were practically rattling the window with your snoring, too."

I crossed my arms and leaned against the counter across from him. "I'm not buying your story. I think you just wanted to get your hands on me."

Justin walked over to me and caged me with his arms. The muscles in his arms flexed, and he smiled showing a dimple I didn't know he had. "If I wanted to get my hands on you, I could have had that when we were alone last week."

My breath stuttered out. "Um . . . I don't know about that."

Justin leaned over and caught my earlobe between his teeth. Lightning shot down right to my core. I bit my lip to keep from moaning. His breathless voice caressed my ear, "You know how badly I want to pull that lip into my mouth and sooth it with my tongue. Every time you do that you make it hard to think of anything but your mouth."

It took all I had to keep my knees from buckling. Opening my eyes, I saw Justin now standing across from me with his muscular arms crossed and a pleased smirk on his face.

I huffed and walked out of the kitchen.

"Don't go too far. Dinner is about ready." His voice had cocky tone that made me want to throat punch him or strip him naked and ride him like I was in the rodeo.

CHAPTER 13

*D*inner with Justin was one of the best meals I had ever had cooked for me. The homemade pasta and sauce was restaurant worthy. His bread had me moaning as it melted on my tongue. Dessert was a decadent chocolate cheesecake. My taste buds were begging me to marry this man.

"How the hell do you know how to make a meal like this?"

"Remember when I said I have many layers?" I nodded. "This is one of my layers. I took classes at a culinary institute when I was getting my MBA. I didn't know if I really wanted to be a CEO or a chef."

"I am impressed."

Justin sat back and crossed his arms. "Glad I could finally impress you. You are awfully hard to please."

Snorting up the water I was drinking made me cough. "What?"

"You are a hard lady to impress. I mean it seems like whenever I get around you things go to hell. First, you drank too much to remember me. Then I was almost a half hour late for our first date. We can't possibly forget the disaster that was the animal shelter and massaging the cat's anal glands." He shrugged helplessly. "I haven't exactly been able to put my best foot forward. I am not used to that."

I stood up from the table and walked over to his chair. Pulling his chair out, I sat on his lap and circled my arms around his neck. Taking his lips in a sweet kiss turned heated very quickly. I broke the kiss and looked him in the eye.

"You have impressed me for a long time. I wanted to get the nerve up to talk to you when you would come into Two Beans and a Latte."

"Really? You never made eye contact with me. I thought you were shy. I know differently now," he snorted.

"I am fucking charming, and you know it."

"Yes."

Kiss

"You"

Kiss

"Are"

Kiss

I grinned at the gorgeous man in front of me and took his face in my hands. "What's next?"

"Movie?"

"Sure. Do you have one in mind?"

"Well, since its getting closer to Christmas why don't we watch one of the best Christmas movies ever?"

"*It's a Wonderful Life*?"

"Nope," he said, walking with me back to his living room.

"*The Grinch*?"

"Nope."

"It's gotta be *A Christmas Story* then."

"You are so cold you're freezing."

I frowned while watching him search through a cabinet I hadn't noticed earlier. "I give up."

He sprang up from his squatting position holding a DVD case. "*Die Hard*!"

"That's not a freaking Christmas movie."

"Of course it is." He started putting it in the player but stopped and looked at me. "You're ok with this movie, right?"

"Sure. If I get bored I can always look around at your pretty Christmas lights."

Justin had a quizzical look on his face and looked around. "I don't have any decorations up, yet."

"Way to go, Captain Obvious. If you want to hang out with me, you better start picking up on sarcasm better." I plopped down on the couch, and Rascal jumped up putting his head in my lap giving me puppy eyes.

Justin put the movie in and walked over to the couch. "Down, Ras."

Rascal ignored him and continued to enjoy my petting.

"Down, Ras," he said more sternly.

This time Rascal lifted his head, looked at Justin and then laid back down. I began laughing at the frustrated look on Justin's face.

"Come on, Ras. I want to cuddle with the girl."

Rascal gave zero fucks about what Justin wanted. Finally, Justin resigned himself to just sitting next to me with Rascal between us.

"So much for my cuddle time," Justin grumbled.

"Oh quit it. If you are lucky, Rascal will get bored and jump down. Then you can put your head in my lap."

Justin cocked an eyebrow and looked at me.

Shit! My brain really needs to keep up with my mouth.

"Not like that you pervert."

"I bet you wouldn't protest if I did."

"Shh. The movie is starting."

Justin's hand caressed my cheek. I rubbed my face against his palm like a cat preening for attention. "So lovely."

CHAPTER 14

*R*ascal didn't move for the entirety of *Die Hard*. Justin and I managed to hold hands throughout the movie. I could feel myself relaxing with him. He was truly a genuine guy. Not at all what anyone would think a billionaire CEO would be like, though I didn't get to see his whole house. He could still have a red room of pain. Why did that thought get me excited?

Our date night didn't end with mad, passionate sex like either of us would have liked. It was more like making out for a half an hour with some over the shirt boob action. I worked at Two Beans in the morning, and Justin had plans he wouldn't elaborate on.

After one last passionate kiss, Sam drove me to my apartment. I walked to my door in a haze. Making sure to be as quiet as possible, I didn't need another night with Mrs. B and her terrorist cat.

In my apartment, I kicked my heels off and headed off to my room. I looked around my apartment and realized I hadn't decorated for Christmas yet. My Gran would have had a fit if she saw how dull it was.

My Gran loved Christmas. Her tree went up on Thanksgiving and stayed up until the second week in January. It was always immaculately decorated. She would have special candles, tablecloths, curtains, plates, napkins, snowmen, angels, and nativity scenes. She had so many nativity scenes. My mom inherited all 50 of those nativity scenes when she passed away.

Gran passed away only a few months ago. Christmas didn't feel the same this year without her. How could I have the same kind of spirit when the lady that put the meaning in the holiday wasn't around anymore? Taking in a deep breath, I wiped my face. My hand came away wet. I didn't even realize I had been crying remembering my Gran.

Walking away from my dark living room and into my bedroom, I put on my flannel PJ's and curled under my covers. Memories flooded my mind of my Gran. Most surrounded Christmas, but all were good. She may have been sassy and didn't take shit from anyone, but when it came to Christmas, she was a big softy. I finally drifted off to sleep thinking about making Christmas cookies with her.

"I AM NOT WEARING THAT."

"Cierra, its part of this year's uniform." Dean passed out the offending objects.

"I think they are cute." Team player Meg perked up.

"It looks like a giant penis. I am not wearing it." Crossing my arms, I dropped the offending object on the counter.

"It does not look like a penis. It is clearly a Christmas tree," Dean protested.

"You made these, didn't you?"

"Of course he did, sweetie," Sean walked over to Dean and rubbed his back.

The kitchen door swung open, and Dinah walked in carrying a tray of pastries. She stopped dead in her tracks when she saw what Meg had on her head. "What in the holy hell do you have on your head?"

"It's a Christmas tree headband." Dean placed one on his head to demonstrate how it was supposed to be worn. It didn't make it any better. It looked like a limp green penis with Christmas lights.

"No, it is not." Dinah took her phone out and took a picture of her brother.

"Dinah, you can go now." Dean shooed her away.

"That is one hell of a Pinterest fail, Dean." Turning and looking at me, Dinah said, "Good luck getting laid when you have a limp Christmas penis on your head."

"DINAH!" Dean freaked out and chased her through the kitchen.

"Christmas penis." Sean cocked his head and stared at Meg. "She's not wrong, but I have to go along with it. So, you guys have to go along with it."

"Fan-freaking-tastic." I grabbed the Christmas penis headband and wore it like a limp unicorn horn. If I had to wear the damn thing, I was going to sport it the way I wanted.

Two Beans and a Latte was seriously busy. The closer we got to the holiday, the more traffic the shop would get. It was three weeks until Christmas and people came in carrying bags from various stores and needed a pick-me-up with a hot coffee. The revolving door of customers was a blur. Fifteen minutes before my shift ended, the crowd finally slowed.

I was busy cleaning the counter and restocking the cups when a woman in a very expensive outfit walked up. Her hair was light gray and styled in a natural wave around her face. Her Coach purse, Christian Louboutin boots, and long Chanel jacket told me all I needed to know. This woman had more money than I will make in my lifetime.

"Can I help you?"

She stared at the Christmas penis on my head and scrunched up her face in distaste.

"Do you know how to make a good latte?" she asked haughtily.

"Yes, ma'am."

"Ok. I will take one of them." She then turned to the person behind her. I hadn't noticed anyone with her until now. My jaw dropped when my eyes met Justin's.

He stared me, holding back a smile. "I will take a coffee with one sugar."

My face felt like it was on fire. Immediately looking down at the register I told the woman the total and tried my best to ignore Justin.

She passed me her black credit card. I did a double take. This was one of those cards that had no limit. She really was loaded.

Handing her card back to her, I turned to help Meg make their order. Before I could though, a hand touched my arm.

"Hey babe." Justin said overly sweetly.

I cleared my throat and smiled at him.

"So, why do you have a limp green penis on your head? Is this a Christmas tradition I don't know about?"

I opened my mouth to rail at him, but the older woman cut me off. "Justin, leave the girl alone. Let her make our drinks so we can leave this place." Her face was screwed up in distaste again.

Justin ignored her. "When do you get off today?"

"Fifteen minutes."

"Good. We need to talk about the ball and some strings I've pulled." He had his sexy smirk on his face, and I tried not to swoon.

Handing them their drinks, I watched as Justin took a seat at a near by table, but the woman went to leave. Walking back to Justin, she looked to be upset with him. They were arguing quietly.

"What's going on over there?" Dean snuck up next to me to watch the scene unfolding.

"No clue, but she is a snotty bitch."

"Yeah. I heard how she acted about this place. Just because we aren't overpriced and fancy doesn't mean we can't make kick-ass coffee." I agreed with Dean.

"It's about that time. I will see you guys next week." Kissing Dean on the cheek, I pulled my apron and headband off walking back to the break room.

Handbag and jacket in tow, I approached Justin's table. It was quiet and very tense.

"You wanted to talk to me?" Standing awkwardly, I looked at Justin and tried to ignore the stare of the woman with him.

Justin jumped up and took me in a tight hug. I was so shocked I couldn't react. I didn't know we were at the PDA part of our relationship. When he pulled back and then kissed me showing just how much he missed me, there was no question how he felt about

PDA. Whistles and catcalls broke our little passion bubble. Blushing, I moved out of his grasp and looked at him.

Taking a deep breath, Justin put his arm around my waist and pointed us toward the woman seated at the table. "Mom, this is Cierra Jameson. Cierra, this is my mother, Vivienne Remington."

Kill me now! Justin's mom saw me with a limp green Christmas penis on my head.

CHAPTER 15

*J*ustin's mom sniffed and put her hand out. I shook it, but it felt like shaking hands with a dead fish. Her grimace stayed on her face as I took a seat next to Justin. He kept his arm around the back of my chair while looking completely relaxed and smug.

"Cierra, I brought my mother here with me because she is on many committees throughout the city, and I thought we could work together with her on this."

"Justin, I told you I didn't think this was going to be something we could do. A small little shelter isn't something that my friends and associates would find worthy of their time or money." Vivienne Remington sipped her latte and refused to look at me.

"Mom! Give us a chance. This is a wonderful place. I volunteered there last weekend and this small sanctuary in the city is fantastic."

She rolled her eyes, then sat up and squinted her eyes at her son. "You volunteered there?"

"Yes. It was one of the best experiences I have ever had." I snapped my head to look at him. I know I had at WTF look on my face.

"Justin, we are not the volunteering in person kind of people. We give money."

"Maybe we should be volunteering in person. That way we can make a connection with the charities we give to, and we can see first-hand the people we help with that money."

Vivienne's lips were in a thin line and her eyes snapped to me. "This is your doing, isn't it?"

I blinked at her angry accusation. Her anger at the idea of her son volunteering for a charity told me a lot about her. She only did charity work because it made her look good in the eyes of society. Volunteering and charity were really four letter words to her. People like me who did it because they cared were beneath her. I decided right then that whether she was Justin's mom or not, I was going to hold my head high. Vivienne Remington's opinion would not phase me.

"Yes, ma'am. Justin wanted to spend time with me, and it happened to be the day I volunteered at the Ride A Horse animal shelter."

"What do you want with my son?"

"Mother!" Justin yelled.

"Justin, do you know anything about this woman? She has clearly had an influence on you. She's made you reckless, tactless and has you acting like a commoner."

"Wow! Mother, I cannot believe you are acting like this. I know it has been hard on you losing dad, but you are acting like such a snob. You don't know Cierra." Justin looked at me while bringing my hand up to his lips. "She is important to me. I've never felt like this with any of those flighty debutantes you tried to fix me up with."

Vivienne looked at me. "Could you please excuse us for a minute, Sara?"

"Her name is Cierra and no she will not be leaving us. She is my girlfriend, Mother. I care about what she cares about. I was hoping you'd be willing to help us in our crusade in helping a very special charity. But, clearly you are only interested in yourself." Justin shook his head, looking dejected. I squeezed his hand that was still in mine.

"How dare you talk to me like that, young man! I will leave you here with your gutter trash." Vivienne Remington stood to leave. "Remember when she steals all your money and ruins your reputation, I told you to stay away from people like that."

All I heard was Vivienne's heels on the café's tiled floor. The patrons sitting at the tables around us were watching the show closely. We were so engrossed in our conversation that I hadn't even noticed that the whole café fell silent. Dean and Sean stood at the counter area looking like they had some choice words sitting on the tips of their tongues.

"I'm sorry." Justin stared at this hand entwined with mine.

"It wasn't your fault." I smiled trying to lift his spirits.

"I had an idea she was going to react that way. Ever since my dad died, she has been acting like that. I don't know why she's acting like such a haughty bitch."

Shaking my head, I said, "Everyone deals with grief differently. She is still struggling."

"My sister warned me not to do this. I figured all she had to do was meet you, so you could talk about the shelter. She wouldn't even give you the time of day."

"Well, her first impression of me wasn't great. She did see me with a Christmas penis on my head."

"IT IS NOT A CHRISTMAS PENIS!" Dean shouted from behind the cash register. The tables around us started to laugh when Dean put one of the headbands on to illustrate his point. Unfortunately, it only illustrated mine.

Justin let out a sad laugh. "That is true, but I'm still sorry. I was hoping she would have been more open to the shelter and to you."

"She is just looking out for her baby boy."

"I don't know why you are defending her. What she just did was indefensible."

Leaning over, I kissed him on the cheek. "I am not defending her, but I can understand grief and how that can change a person. Maybe the next time will be a better meeting, and we can just ignore this disaster." I tilted my head toward Dean and Sean with their headbands on.

"Oh, we are never letting that go. But, I guess you are right. We can try the introduction again another time." He had a devilish look on his face when he looked at me. "Next time, no Christmas penis."

"You have a deal. Now, let's go grab some Chinese and watch one of the documentaries I've wanted to watch on Netflix."

"That sounds great." Grabbing my hand, he pulled me out of my seat

"HOW CAN YOU WATCH THESE THINGS?" Justin tilted his head at the screen.

"True crime documentaries?" Justin nodded and took another bite of his fried rice. "I love these things. It has me guessing, disgusted, sad, happy and mad all in the span of an hour and a half. Plus, in the end I get to decide if I think what they portrayed was true."

Justin looked pensively at me. "Any other documentaries you like?"

"I love history docs. Those make history so fun and interesting. I never really liked history or political science in school but when I watch a World War II documentary, I get sucked in and with those I feel like I really learned something."

"Now, that sounds like it is right up my alley. Can't we put one of those on?" He reached for the remote, but I was quicker and held it away from him.

"No! We are going to find out about this cult and what happened to the people in it."

Justin looked at me and took my sweet and sour chicken off my lap. Placing it on the coffee table in front of us, he crawled over and laid on me.

Justin cupped my face. His lips met mine in a sweet, gentle kiss. He pulled back and stared into my eyes. They sparkled with something I couldn't decipher. The sexy grin he wore popped his dimple. I was about to melt into a pile of goo if he kept looking at me like that. He kissed me again with more urgency. Our moans mingled together when I ran my hands through his hair.

Justin jerked upright so quick my eyes took a minute to adjust. He had a devilish grin. In his hands was my remote. "Now, let's see about these war documentaries."

I let out a battle cry as if I was channeling Xena and dove at him. We wrestled for the remote and rolled off the couch onto the floor. The remote was forgotten, and it was now just a tickle battle. Justin managed to pin me on the floor with my hands above my head. He straddled my hips while I tried to squirm away.

"I wouldn't keep doing that if I were you. You are giving me ideas." He pressed his chest against mine while keeping a light grip on my wrists.

Cocking my eyebrow, I rolled my hips. "Maybe I want you to have ideas."

"Hmm." He said inching closer to my mouth.

Bang. Bang. Bang.

I jolted up and rammed my forehead into his nose.

"Oh, fuck!" Justin rolled over to the side and held his nose.

"Oh my God! Are you ok?" I lifted his hands and took a look at his face. Blood was streaming down his nose. "Let me get you a towel and ice."

Bang. Bang. Bang.

Jumping up, I called toward the door. "I'll be right there."

Rummaging through my cabinets, I found a dish cloth. I took a handful of ice and placed it in the towel.

"Here you go. Tilt your head back. Let me see who is at the door."

Marching over to the door I yanked it open. The words vomited out before I could stop them. "What the hell do you wa—"

"Well, hello to you, Cierra."

Color drained from my face. "Mom?"

CHAPTER 16

"*A*ren't you going to invite us in?"

"Dad is with you too?" The hall was empty behind her.

"Oh yes, the nice old lady across the hall needed help with something." She barged in, took her coat off, and dropped her purse on my table.

My mother gave my apartment a cursory look and frowned. "You haven't decorated."

"I haven't had time, yet."

She turned and looked at me. "I know it is going to be hard for you this year. With your Gran no longer here, it's tough on me too." Her eyes glistened with tears while her lip quivered.

I then did something I hadn't done since I was ten. I hugged my mom really tight. Feeling her shake broke my heart. I may have lost my Gran, but she lost her mom. Rubbing her back, I tried to sooth her.

The door banged open and my dad came marching in. "I am never helping that woman again. Don't even try to guilt me about this, Margaret. She had me holding some cat that she kept calling an asshole while she tried to force it to take some medication. My arms are scratched all to hell. She is a wack-a-doodle!" My dad continued his march over to my couch and plopped down. "AHHH!"

"What now, Jerry?" My mom gave an exasperated sigh.

"There is someone laying on this couch." My dad looked at me, pointing to the couch. "Do you know someone is laying on the couch holding a towel to their face?"

For a second, I had completely forgot Justin was still here. "No, Dad! Who the hell is that? We have been having problems with vagrants following people into their apartments, laying on their couches and stealing towels."

My parents stared at me for a moment. It was my dad that responded the quickest. "Don't be a smart-ass to the master. I taught you how to be one. Who is this?"

Biting back a laugh, I walked over to the couch and helped Justin sit up. "Well, this is Justin. He's my . . . uh . . . friend."

Dad looked at Justin and then back to me. "Finally getting laid?"

"JERRY!" My mom squealed.

"What, Margaret? You are always complaining that all your friends have grandbabies but not you. That you . . . and I quote . . . . "'Wish Cierra would just get laid and have babies. Accident or no is fine with you.'"

My mother's face caught fire. "I would . . . uh . . . never say that."

"Bullshit." My dad said, sitting next to Justin. He stuck his hand out to him. "Jerry Jameson, Cierra's dad."

Justin shook his hand while trying to keep the ice on his face. "Justin Remington, Cierra's boyfriend."

"BOYFRIEND?" My mom squealed again.

"Good Christ, Margaret. Turn the volume down." My mom flipped my dad the bird and turned to me.

"He calls us boyfriend/girlfriend. I haven't agreed yet."

She looked at me blankly then took my arm and dragged me into the kitchen. "What do you mean you haven't agreed yet?"

I went about unloading my dishwasher so she couldn't see my face. "I don't know, Mom." Pausing I looked back at her, "He seems almost too good to be true."

"He is quite the cutie, but he doesn't seem to be crazy or out of your league. Why are you scared?"

"I'm NOT scared." I banged the cabinets.

"Can one of you make us sandwiches?" My dad yelled from my couch. He and Justin were watching what looked to be a World War II documentary.

Ignoring them, my mom picked up utensils to put away. "Yes you are. I just don't understand why."

How could I tell her that I wasn't really sure I knew how to care for another person? She didn't need to know that I was worried about if we didn't work out, and I'd lose one of the best jobs I've ever had. Worse, I was worried if it did work out. We came from two different worlds. I'd never fit in his.

"Honey, why are you staring at Justin like that?"

Blinking, I dazedly looked at my mom. "How was I looking at him?"

"You were looking at him like you either wanted to take him to your room and make a man out of him or let him go."

I just looked at my mom.

"I'm fine."

Mom gave me a sad smile.

"Margaret! Sandwich Now! We men are hungry!" My dad yelled again and this time punctuated it with fists pounding on his chest.

"Can it, Jerry. If you and Justin are hungry, get your asses up and make something yourself."

"For the record, I am not hungry." Mumbling just loud enough to be heard, Justin looked directly at me.

"Don't puss out on me now, Justin." Dad had never been a subtle man, but his staged whispers were the worst.

Mom's eyes rolled around so hard in her head, I think she saw the back of her head.

"Hold on a minute." My arms were crossed, and I glared at mom. "Why are you no longer speaking in a British accent?"

Mom perked up. "They decided not to do *A Streetcar Named Desire*. We are now putting on *Rent*."

I blinked.

"I'm going to read for the part of the angel."

What the hell was she talking about? "There is no angel in that musical. Are you sure your community theatre wants to put that on?"

"There is definitely an angel. Why wouldn't we put on *Rent*?"

I shook my head. "Ok. First, Angel is the name of a character not a celestial being. Second, he is a gay man who likes to dress in women's clothing. Third, you live in an incredibly religious town. They want to do a musical about AIDS, homosexuality and drugs?"

"That isn't what that's about. It's about a group of people who need to pay rent and they sing songs about what kind of work they do to pay for it. It is a sweet story."

My mom couldn't be this naïve. "Uh nope."

She sighed and looked at me. When a thought occurred to her, she perked up. "Want to hear me sing my audition piece?"

"Sure. What are you singing?"

"The song is a bit dated and dirty."

"Ok, Mom. Just do it."

From the kitchen I saw my dad hand Justin something. Then turned the captions on the TV.

"I'm going to sing *I Kissed a Girl* by Katy Perry."

My jaw hit the floor. "Wha—"

Mom grabbed the ladle off the counter and began singing into it.

To say my mom sung badly was an understatement. Her voice was a mix between the mating call of a moose and a cat getting its tail caught in a door. I looked over at Justin and my dad. They sat completely still facing the TV.

"Ok, Mom." My voice carried over her "singing".

Her final note carried on way too long. She smiled and looked very proud of herself.

"What do you think?"

"Uh . . . so why are you and dad here?"

Confusion crossed her face. "I thought I said. We came to do some holiday things with you. Clearly, you need to decorate. We will get you set up."

Sudden warmth enveloped me. "Baking cookies too?"

"Of course, sweetie." My mom pulled me into a hug that almost made me forget her horrible rendition of *I Kissed A Girl*.

CHAPTER 17

"*D*id you see Justin today?" Trina asked from my office door.

"Yep." I forced all of my concentration on the paper in front of me.

"Do you know what happened to his face?"

I shrugged and continued to skim the document in front of me. It was the third time I'd read the same paragraph. My focus had been horrible since the impromptu visit of my parents.

"Are you listening to me?" Trina asked.

Before I could answer, Janice poked her head into my office. "Cierra, Mr. Remington asked that you meet him at 12 for a lunch to discuss the charity ball you are working on."

"Thanks, Janice."

Trina stood silently waiting for Janice to be out of earshot. "Business lunch? Is that code for screwing on his desk?"

I choked on my coffee. "What? Are you channeling Dinah now?"

She cocked an eyebrow at me. "Well, why else would he need to have a 'business lunch'?" Lifting her hands in air quotes for business lunch.

"Look, I didn't tell you this but Ride A Horse may be closing its doors if they don't get a lot of money before January 1st," I said. "Justin happened to be there when I found out. We talked to Jonas about having a charity ball between Christmas and New Years. I'm guessing he wants to talk about the plans I have to pull this together is less than three weeks."

"Oh no! Obie and Artie could possibly have to go to a kill shelter."

I nodded.

"You could always adopt them."

"Hell, no! I love those two horny bastards, but you know I couldn't adopt even one dog let alone two."

"I know, Trina. Just cross your fingers I can pull this off."

"I have faith in you," Trina checked her watch. "I will leave you alone to prep for your lunch with the boss man." I rolled my eyes at her.

I APPROACHED Justin's assistant's desk. "Can I help you?"

"Ms. Jameson to see Mr. Remington."

She cracked her gum and looked up at me for the first time. "Go ahead. He's in there."

I approached his door nervously. Wiping my hands on my pencil skirt, I did a quick check of myself in the mirrored door-jamb. It was like looking at myself in a funhouse mirror, but at least I could tell I didn't look a total wreck.

Knocking softly, I waited to hear his voice.

All I heard was silence on the other side. I glanced back to his assistant who was now filing her nails and popping her gum.

I knocked a bit louder. Still nothing.

Not knowing what else to do, I tried the doorknob. It turned easily and I walked in.

The office I walked into felt like one straight out of *Mad Men*. It was a dated décor. A giant mahogany desk sat in the middle of the office. Uncomfortable-looking chairs faced it. A black leather sofa sat diagonally from the desk on my right. An incredible amount of light flowed in from floor to ceiling windows behind the desk.

A door creaked open on my left, and Justin walked in. Surprise colored his expression.

"Hi." He looked at me sheepishly. His tie was loosened, and he was without a suit jacket. His face looked like he'd been in the practice ring with Rocky. No wonder Trina freaked out when she saw it.

"You wanted to see me, Mr. Remington?" With my shoulders back, notepad under my arm and a practiced blank look on my face, I attempted to look professional.

From the look on his face, I failed miserably. "You don't have to call me Mr. Remington."

"I feel that we should keep our office and private relationships separate."

Justin looked at me blankly.

"Did you want to talk to me about Ride A Horse?"

He walked over to his desk and proceeded to put his suit jacket back on and tightened his tie. He'd pressed the intercom while I stood there like a dumbfounded statue.

"Ms. McCoy, could you please call downstairs and have my and Ms. Jameson's lunch brought up?"

"Yes, Mr. Remington."

"Please have a seat, Cierra. It may take a bit for our lunch to come so we should start outlining what we can and cannot do for this. Ms. McCoy is a temp. My actual assistant just got married."

"Ok."

For the next 15 minutes, Justin and I outlined the ball. We wanted it to be elegant but simple too. Dinner would be served. He wanted to be sure that some of the animals came in with hopes of either being adopted or drumming up donors who wouldn't be able to say no to a sweet puppy or kitten.

I feverishly took notes. In the margins, I jotted down my personal contacts and strings I felt I could pull from my internship at another event planning agency. Whenever there was a lull in the conversation, my mind would wander to the sexy man in front of me and wondered what that leather couch would feel like under my exposed ass while he licked me.

"Cierra, did you get that?" Justin was looking at me as if I had a weird look on my face.

"Huh?"

"I asked if you'd like to have lunch on the couch."

"Oh . . . uhm . . . sure."

He picked up the brown sacks that were not there a second ago. I blinked at them and wondered how long I could have possibly been daydreaming.

I stood up and straightened my skirt.

Justin sat on the couch placing the two bags between us. I sat on the cushion across from him and opened the bag. It was a basic brown paper bag lunch that contained a sandwich, chips, diet soda, and a cookie.

"Fancy." I took a bite of the sandwich and moaned. This was going to easily be the best brown bag lunch I'd ever had.

His eyes met mine when he took a bite. His moan sent an excited chill down my spine. We ate in silence and after a few minutes, it started to feel awkward.

Justin wiped his mouth and looked at me. "Why are things awkward now?"

"They aren't awkward," I lied.

"You are a horrible liar. Now, tell me what is going on."

I shoved a handful of chips in my mouth buying myself a few seconds to think.

He raised an eyebrow in question.

I took a quick drink and a deep breath. "I don't know, Justin. I thought it would be a good idea to keep everything separate. But, this is just so difficult."

"It doesn't have to be difficult." He cleared our lunches and pulled me toward him. Wrapping his arms around me, I melted into his warmth.

"Don't you think it will look bad though? I don't want people to think I got this position because I'm sleeping with the boss."

He snorted. "We haven't even slept together yet." He kissed my hair. "I'd like to remedy that very soon."

I stared into his eyes and felt myself falling. I knew now was a good time I should say something sweet or seductive. "Your face looks a mess." That was neither.

Justin grinned then grimaced. "You aren't the first person to tell me that."

I ran my hands over his stubbled jaw. "You're still incredibly handsome. You could be a model if you ever wanted to give up the CEO gig."

"Really? You think so?"

Leaning back, I looked him over in a dramatic fashion. "Well not today, but once your pretty face heals."

Justin pulled me into his lap and kissed me hard. Melting into his kiss, I let my hands wander over his jacket-covered arms. I felt his hands flex on my waist.

"Get your hands off my fiancée!" A shrill voice rang from the office door.

CHAPTER 18

*J*ustin and I startled pulling away from each other. We looked at the door and a beautiful woman with long black hair, a cream sheath dress, skyscraper heels, and an open winter jacket stood with her hands on her hips. Her blood red lips were pursed into a line. She was impeccable compared to me.

"Sicora?" Justin questioned.

"We thought we'd surprise you and take you to lunch, darling." She glided over to Justin, who was now standing in front of me.

"We?"

"Yes, Justin. We." His mother said from behind the bombshell.

I stood quickly and nervously fixed my clothes.

"Hello, Sara," Vivienne said smugly. "Have you met Sicora Reynolds, Justin's fiancée?"

I forced myself to straighten up and look at the women. Sicora glared at me. In one look, I knew what she saw. I was nothing but a gnat in her world. Their disgusted looks made me feel like I was dirt on one of their stilettos.

Vivienne was clearly getting a sick enjoyment out of my discomfort. Nodding with a tight smile I said, "Good to see you again, Mrs. Remington."

"I can't say the same."

"Justin, can you tell your toy to leave now? We have important wedding plans to discuss." Sicora ran her hand down the front of his chest.

I walked briskly over to the desk where my file and notepad sat.

"Cierra, wait."

"Mr. Remington, I will work on the rest of the details for the ball and send a report of my work to your assistant by the end of the day. Thank you for lunch." I refused to look at Justin.

I BARELY MADE it to the restroom when salty tears slid down my cheeks. I shut myself in one of the stalls and cried silently. Justin Remington was engaged. He had lied to me this entire time. No wonder his mother was so rude to me. I was a home wrecker in her eyes or worse yet a gold digger after her son.

I was silently sobbing into my hands when I heard the bathroom door open. I pulled my legs up so whoever it was didn't see me in there.

"Oh my God! Can you believe it?" A familiar voice squealed.

"I know. I knew she had to have been screwing someone to get her position."

An icy finger slid down my spine.

"Janice, you should have seen her face when she walked out of Remington's office. It was great." The familiar voice said. I looked through the small opening and saw it was Justin's temp with my assistant Janice. They were fixing their make-up in the mirror.

"I wish I'd have been there. She took that job right out from under me. I'm glad you just let Mrs. Remington and Ms. Reynolds in there without warning. I hope you won't get into trouble."

"So, what if I get into trouble. I can't stand this job anyway."

"We better get back. I can't wait to spread this around. She's gonna hate it here." Janice had a dark smile on her face.

"I love when you get evil, cousin."

The two of them left. I put my legs down and felt the tears coming all over again. Letting myself wallow for a few minutes longer and then took some deep breaths and left the stall.

"I'll be damned if the Remingtons are going to hurt me." I mumbled to my reflection in the mirror. "I can do this."

After checking my appearance one last time in the mirror, I strode out of the bathroom and back to my office.

The rest of my day flew by. I threw myself into my work by keeping my door shut and ignoring my emails. Before I left for the day, I checked my email and saw twenty from Justin. I ignored and deleted them in case someone would hack my inbox.

By the time I left for the day, everyone was gone. I hadn't realized that I had worked well past five. The short elevator ride down to the lobby let me continue to think about everything that had happened during my day. I forced myself to focus, but Justin kept creeping into my thoughts.

The ding of the elevator forced me out of my thoughts. The clacking of my heels was the only noise echoing through the lobby. Our security guard looked up and smiled.

"Have a good night, Ben." I said.

"You too, Ms. Jameson." He had a funny smile on his face and looked toward the couches in the lobby.

Justin was sitting on the couch looking at his phone. He looked up and stood quickly. Striding over to me, he had a panicked look on his face.

"Cierra." He stopped a few feet in front of me.

"Mr. Remington." I nodded and walked around him toward the door.

"Please." He grabbed my arm as I strode by.

Willing myself to have no reaction to his touch, I stopped and looked at the door.

"Let me explain," Justin pleaded.

"I don't think that is necessary, Mr. Remington. You have a fiancée. I didn't need to know for what you wanted to use me for. It's fine. I'm over it."

"You're wrong. Let me take you to dinner, and we can talk. It's all a big misunderstanding."

I closed my eyes. The pain in my chest had tears stinging my eyes. I would not let Justin see me cry. "I don't think that is wise, Mr. Remington. Now, if that is all, I'd like to get home. I've had a challenging day." My voice had as much ice as I could muster in it.

"This is not fucking all, Cierra. I am not done with you or with us."

My body began to shake as the dam holding back my emotions started to crack. "Please." I begged softly.

We made eye contact in the window. His sad eyes were hurting as much as mine. He nodded, and I walked out into the cold December night.

CHAPTER 19

"**W**hy haven't we seen Justin around?" My mom asked while adding flour to the batter mixture.

I had decided not to tell my parents about what happened with us. My mom would want me to try to find a way to be with him, and my dad would ask where I wanted him to bury the body. Neither would have been helpful for the heartache I had. Only Trina and Dinah knew, and we were going to bar tonight.

"He's been busy." A plume of flour shot up into my face, and I coughed. "Be careful, mom."

"Sorry, sweetie. You know I was never the baker. Your gran was always the one who did that." Her sad smile tore at my heart in a whole other way.

"It's ok. I inherited Gran's baking skills."

The next few hours, mom and I baked until we were tired. Dad would sneak in and try each cookie. Giving them all his enthusiastic thumbs up. I was finishing up the last batch of butter cookies when my doorbell rang. Assuming it was Mrs. Buchanan, I answered the door without looking through the peephole.

A huge floral arrangement was staring me in the face. The teenager holding it awkwardly looked at me then at his paperwork.

"Ms. Cierra Jameson?"

"That's me," I confirmed.

"These are for you." He handed me the vase then turned to walk away.

"Thank you." My voice was muffled by the flowers.

"Wait. There are more." I blinked at him not comprehending what the teenager was saying.

"More?"

"Yep. There are ten more arrangements."

"Who's at the door?" Mom stood next to me. "Oh my, those are nice." She took them out of my hands and brought them into my apartment.

"Look lady, can I bring the rest up here?"

"Sure. The door will be ajar. You can just put them over there." I showed him where there was space along my wall.

The flower delivery boy made seven trips in and out of the apartment. Each bouquet was larger than the last. Roses of every color, lilies, daisies and carnations came in artistically arranged bunches. By the time the boy was done, I felt I should offer him a tip. All I got from him was a "taken care of."

My apartment was now a flower shop. I could guess whom they were from, but I wanted to pretend it wasn't from him. Justin must have bought out the entire flower shop.

"Any idea who they are from?" I hated when my mom asked me a sneaky question that she knew the answer to. So, to be difficult I just shrugged and went back into the kitchen to finish the cookies.

"Margaret, you know damn well it's from that boy. He must have fucked up royally." Dad stole two more cookies and wove his way through the many vases.

"Language, Jerry!"

"Mom, you know who these are from, but it doesn't matter. I'm not talking to him no matter how many flowers he sends." The door-bell rang just to punctuate my point.

I swung the door open and saw an older gentleman standing in front of me. "Can I help you?"

"Ms. Cierra Jameson?"

"Yes."

"Ok." He turned and yelled to someone down the hall. "Bring it in here along with all the bags." He looked back at me and asked, "May we please come in?"

"What for? What is all this about?"

"We have a delivery. We have been paid generously to set up everything."

"What are you delivering?" What the hell had Justin done now?

"This." He pointed to a giant Christmas tree that was being dragged down my hall. Behind the two people with the tree, were three more people carrying bags from high-end stores.

"Uh . . . ok."

"What is happening now?" My mother barged toward the door and almost got a face full of pine tree. I would have laughed if I weren't completely dumb founded.

We watched as this group of professionals set up the tree, decorated it with new expensive ornaments and lights. While some were working on the tree, others were busy hanging lights, signs, wreaths, and any other Christmas decoration that was possible. An hour later, I was thanking them and ushering them out of the apartment.

The apartment now looked incredibly elegant and Christmasy. Each of the floral bouquets was incorporated seamlessly in the design of all the decorations. They were clearly planned as part of the surprise.

"What the hell happened here?" Dad turned around from the couch and looked at me like he was in another world.

"What, dad?"

"Did you and your mother do this?" He waved his arm around at the apartment.

"No . . . there were just a bunch of people here doing it the past hour," my mom said. "Where the hell were you?"

"I was sitting here watching the game."

"Bullshit! You fell asleep with those earplugs in, didn't you?" I crossed my arms blurting out my father's secret.

"Wha— uh no," he stuttered.

"Earplugs?" Damn! My mom could give a ninja a run for their money.

"Dad?" I shrugged. He glared at me, and I smiled my most angelic smile. "I gotta get ready. The girls will be here soon."

Speed-walking over to my bedroom, I could hear the muffled voices of my parents. I giggled while I looked through my closet for something both comfortable and sexy. That didn't exist but I grabbed the next best thing. Glancing at the time, I rushed out of my room, clothes in hand and into my bathroom. Glad my friends were never ones to be on time.

"I CAN'T BELIEVE he did all that." Trina exclaimed over the band playing.

"Yep. I'm not exactly happy about it." I finished my vodka pineapple and stared at the band.

"Oh, please. I'm betting he got your panties wet for that." Trina and I snapped our gazes over to Dinah. She shrugged. "You were thinking it, I am just the loud mouth with no filter who said it."

"You are all that and more." Dean's voice carried over the music. I stood from and pulled him into a hug.

"What the hell are you two doing here?" I reached past Dean and hugged Sean in an equally fierce squeeze.

"A little birdie told us you were going to be here and that you needed some girl time." Dean gestured to him and Sean. "So, here we are."

Dinah rolled her eyes, and Trina giggled.

"This is an awesome surprise. Grab chairs and sit down."

Dean sat next to me slinging his arm over the back of my chair. Sean brought a chair over but gestured going to the bar. Raising my glass, I asked for another.

"Tell me all the gos', girl! Dinah said something about a hotty CEO sending lots of flowers, a Christmas tree, and interior decorators."

I glared over to Dinah. "Well, I know who your little birdie was."

Dean flinched when Dinah expertly kicked her brother in the shin.

"So, spill." Sean said, setting drinks in front of me and Dean.

For the next couple hours, I shared all the drama from work, the gifts, avoiding Justin, my parents and anything else that has been in the maelstrom that was my life. Between stories and drinks we would get up and dance. Weaving through sweaty bodies and groping hands reminded me of how I met Justin for the first time. A pang shot through my heart.

Excusing myself from the throng of dancers, I sat back down at the table and watched my friends dance. Dinah danced provocatively with a guy that was even taller than her that looked like a lumberjack. Dean and Sean took turns spinning Trina around but her eyes kept flitting over to the bar looking for Donny.

"You ok, Cierra?" Donny's voice jolted me out of my thoughts.

"Yep. You must be swamped tonight."

He nodded and replaced my drink with a fresh one. "I didn't order that."

"I know. But, a guy at the bar sat watching you for the past hour. He wanted me to bring this over to you."

It was my vodka pineapple. The bustle of people around my table made it difficult for me to see the guy that Donny was talking about.

"Is he still here, Donny?"

He squinted toward the bar and shook his head. "Someone is sitting where he was. Sorry, Cierra."

I placed my hand on his shoulder and gave it a squeeze. "Thanks, Donny."

"Uh huh." His gaze was caught on Dinah and her dance partner. He was never going to get a clue.

People milled about everywhere. The band was on a break and all the dancers and fans headed toward the bar. I saw a familiar head walking toward the exit. The people in front of me were not moving. I had to get my bitch card out push some people out of the way. Comments and curses were thrown my way. My name was called, but I didn't stop. I needed to see if it was him, and he had some questions he needed to answer.

The crowd thinned out the closer I got to the exit. Smokers left to stand outside the building to smoke any number of things. A cloud of smoke blurred my vision when I walked past the bouncer. Before I was totally away from him, I stuck my hand out for a handstamp to get back in.

Cars were scattered throughout the lot. Thumping music poured out of the building with each new smoker joining the crew outside. I ran to my right and saw a couple kissing in a darkened alcove but not the one person I was looking for.

I ran back to the left and passed in front of the smokers again. The heat from their stares brought my situation into stark color. I was outside a bar, chasing after someone I didn't know if I should be chasing while running around like a lunatic. When reality finally hit, I skidded to a stop. Unfortunately, my heels got caught on some gravel and the next thing I knew I was on my ass with my leg under me.

If my fall wasn't enough to embarrass me, the pain that was now shooting up from my ankle had me on fire. The murmurs of the smokers filtered over to me. I scrambled to get up, but the moment I put any weight on my ankle I crumpled to the ground.

"Don't get up." A deep voice came from the darkness to my left.

"I can't just sit here. I am in a parking lot." I huffed.

"Yes, but you could hurt yourself more."

"I'm used to pain." It came out so soft I didn't know if he'd heard me.

He squatted next to me. "Can I help you, Cierra?"

The soft sweetness of his plea brought tears to my eyes. I sniffed and wiped at my eyes turning away from him. I could do this on my own. I didn't need some man to come and rescue me. My gaze floated down to my ankle. It was starting to look like an oddly shaped balloon animal. I needed ice, and I needed it yesterday.

Justin continued to look at me with the same plea from the lobby in his eyes.

"Alright. Just so you know, I'm only allowing this because I need to get this iced and elevated ASAP. This doesn't mean anything else. Got it?"

"Understood." His hands slipped under my arms and lifted me to my feet. He probably would have carried me, but my anger would have only given him a swift kick to the balls . . .with my bad foot.

Justin escorted me back into the bar. He notified the bouncers about what happened and he took me to where Dinah, Trina, Dean and Sean were sitting. They all looked up when they noticed me limping and hanging on the one man I had just told them I wanted nothing more to do with.

"What the hell happened?" Sean asked taking me from Justin. I nodded thanks and sat in his vacated seat.

"Well, the brakes on these heels don't work very well. So, when I tried to stop my feet got caught up in the gravel and boom . . . graceful fall and instant pain."

"Sweetie, I've told you not to wear heels and run. You have problems walking in sneakers let alone heels. I'm going to have work with you again, aren't I?" Dean sat rubbing my back while he tried to make light of the mood.

"Oh my God! Are you ok?" A breathless Donny handed Sean the ice pack. "Gino said someone got hurt in the parking lot. I didn't think it would be you."

"Then you're an idiot," Dinah said gruffly. "You should have thought it was her as soon as you heard it."

He stood there staring at Dinah and blushed. Moving back toward the bar, I heard a soft "I better get back."

"Why are you so mean to him?" Dean asked. I was grateful for the distraction. As of right now, no one was paying attention to the hot guy, rather the hot *engaged* guy, I never wanted to speak to again was still here.

Dean and Dinah bickered back and forth about her treatment of the "little puppy," as Dean dubbed him. Sean's gaze never left Justin. If looks could kill, Justin would have been dead thirty-three times over by now.

"Trina, can I have an aspirin?"

All heads snapped to me. Admonitions came rapid fire.

"You can't have any medicine you've been drinking."

"You need more than an aspirin."

"Are you trying to kill yourself?"

"I think I have something better."

My head was spinning as the vodka pineapples were finally

kicking in. "You know what, I just want to go home." Forgetting about my ankle, I attempted to stand. When the white, hot pain shot up my leg, I buckled and my butt landed hard in the chair.

"For chrissakes Cierra, why did you do that? I will take you home," Dinah said, reaching for her jacket and purse.

"Wait a minute, all of you have been drinking. I can just call an Uber."

"I can drive you." Justin spoke up for the first time since we came back into the bar.

"Oh hell no, Mr. Sexy. We won't be letting you alone with our girl." Sean spoke up and stood chest-to-chest with Justin.

In a loud stage whisper, Dean said, "He's so sexy when he gets all manly. Makes me all swoony."

Dinah rolled her eyes. "Keep it in your pants, Dean."

"Hold on, you've been drinking too. I'm not going with you." I winced when I moved my leg.

"I haven't had one drop of alcohol tonight." He crossed his muscular arms across his chest. Ugh! I didn't want to notice that or remember the feeling of those around me.

"I don't believe you."

Justin looked at my friends and then back to me. "Fine, I will prove it to you."

He walked over to the bar and got Donny's attention. Arm movements and what looked like pleading from Justin managed to get Donny away from the bar. Donny was clearly uncomfortable and wouldn't look at anyone other than me.

"Cierra, he hasn't had a drop of anything other than water."

I trusted Donny. We have known him for years, and I never thought he'd put me in a position that would cause me harm. But, I had to be the bitch and ask the question. "You aren't just saying that so Justin can get me alone, are you?"

Donny looked like I had physically hit him. "What? Cierra, you know I would never put you in any position that would harm you. Let alone let you get into a car with someone drunk."

"Donny! She had to ask the question. You never know where someone's loyalty lies," Dinah said.

Donny stared at Dinah as if he didn't know her then walked back to the bar without another look toward our table.

"Fine. You can take me home."

Standing wasn't something that was easy for me at the moment. A strong arm wrapped around my waist and I draped my arm around his shoulders. Not leaning in and sniffing him was incredibly challenging. Memories of his arms on me. His lips on mine. My hands in his.

Focus!

I gave myself a mental slap. Meeting his eyes while he helped me out of the bar was a huge mistake. His sexy smirk only told me that accepting this ride was a bad decision.

CHAPTER 20

The pretty car he used for our first date was sitting in the back of the parking lot. He propped me against the wall with the smokers while he went to retrieve it. My ankle had now become a cankle and was throbbing to the beat of a drum.

"Are you sure you want to leave with him?" Trina stood next to me.

"He hasn't been drinking. It will be fine."

"Will it? You could still get an Uber or Lyft or taxi?"

"I am going to pretend he is one of those three and just ignore him. I'm not dumb enough to make the same mistake twice."

Trina patted my shoulder when she saw the headlights approaching. "Oh sweetie, you aren't stupid. You're human, and we all make mistakes when it comes to our hearts. I can see yours in your eyes when you look at him." She looked over at Justin who was getting out of the car. "Don't let him hurt you. Guard your heart." She disappeared back into the bar.

I was still looking at the space where Trina had been standing when Justin came up to me.

"Ready?"

I looked at Justin and then back to the bar. It would be so easy just to say no. End it all right now and never think of him again. My heart ached at that thought. So, I said the only thing I could, "Yes."

Warm air blew on me from the vents in the car. When I was settled in the seat with the seatbelt buckled, I stared out of the window. Justin turned on the radio to Christmas music. The music softly played in the background while I watched houses with Christmas lights and decorations go by.

Justin drove a much more sedate pace. The tension was incredibly obvious in the car. He wanted to talk. I didn't. There was nothing he could say to me that would penetrate this wall I built up.

Who was I kidding . . . his kisses could totally melt that wall as if it was made out of marshmallows.

"Are you ok?"

"Of course. Why would you ask?"

His face pinched at the snappish tone I used. "You were sighing. I thought you might be in pain."

"I am." I said under my breath.

He took a deep breath, pulling the car into an empty church parking lot. Putting the car in park, he unbuckled his seatbelt and turned toward me.

"Alright. Let me have it."

"What?" I continued to stare out the window. "Why did you pull over? I want to go home."

"Cierra, we are going to clear the air. I can't stand this between us."

"There is nothing you can say that will change my mind. Now, please start the car or I will call a cab."

Silence filled the car. I watched the light on the manger in front of the church.

"I'm not engaged, Cierra." He paused waiting for me to have a reaction. I gave him none. "She lied. My mother encouraged her. I'm sorry they hurt you."

Hope blossomed in my chest, but that evil little voice in the back of my head kept saying *Yeah right! He's the one who lied*. That voice beat my hope into submission.

"Why does it matter, Justin?"

He flinched and looked like I had kicked his puppy. "I care about you, that's why it matters."

I rolled my eyes.

"What can I say to get you to believe me?"

"I don't know, Justin. I really don't know why this matters so much to you. We have only known each other for a few weeks."

"Cierra, I care so much about you. You are all I think about anymore. From the first time I walked into Two Beans to the night you almost broke my nose, I have only wanted to be around you more and more." He took my hand in his and rubbed my knuckles with his thumb. "I'm falling for you more and more. Can you honestly say you feel nothing for me?"

I opened my mouth to deny everything he said, but I couldn't. Snapping my mouth shut, my teeth clicked, and I looked out the window watching as snow began to fall.

"I can't say that."

The tension in the car melted away. "Will you let me tell you about Sicora?"

I swallowed and nodded. He squeezed my hand in his and took a deep breath.

"The Reynold's family and mine are very close friends. My mother went to college with Sicora's mother. They were sorority sisters. So, when they both married millionaires, they planned their family's futures together. They even managed to get pregnant around the same time. Sicora and I grew up together. I was her escort for every event whether I wanted to or not." He ran his hands through his hair.

"Last year, we decided to try to be a couple. Our mothers were over-joyed. Honestly, I knew I didn't want a relationship with her. It was purely sexual. After a few months, I broke it off because I didn't think it was fair to either of us to fake feelings neither of us had. Three months ago, Sicora showed up at my apartment and begged me to get back together with her. She begged and cried. I felt bad for her, so I said we could try. It didn't last the month." He looked at me with a sad smile. "I hadn't seen her since then. Except for that horrible incident in my office."

"Why did she say she was your fiancée?"

"Apparently, unbeknownst to me, she told our mothers we were engaged. That was why my mother acted the way she did when she first met you. She thought you were my mistress."

"Does your mother know you weren't engaged?"

He shook his head. "I tried to tell her, but Sicora was crying from me supposedly "ditching her at the altar." She left in a huff with the crying Sicora."

"Ok."

"Ok?"

I turned in my seat and looked into his amazingly beautiful eyes. "What do you want me to say, Justin? I don't know what to believe."

"Believe me! That is what I want you to say. Say you believe me. I'm desperate for it. For you. Can't you see you are the only thing I want this Christmas?" He pulled my hand to his lips then continued.

"For next Christmas."

He placed a soft kiss on my wrist.

"For the Christmas after that."

His lips traveled to the inside of my elbow placing another sweet kiss.

"For all the Christmases."

His travels halted then he leaned in until he was a breath away from my lips.

"What do you want for Christmas?" His breath caressed my lips.

"Everything." The word came out on a breath.

Justin quirked a sexy smile.

"Let me give that to you." In ad movement so swift I didn't know who moved first, I was in his arms kissing him.

His lips were soft and pliant against mine. On a moan, he slipped his tongue inside my mouth. Our tongues battled one another. His hands roamed up my body causing me to shudder. I pulled him closer dying for his warmth and strength. He moved my hips to pull me into his lap. Pain immediately shot through my body. I whimpered, and Justin pulled back.

"Are you ok?" He panted.

"Yes. My ankle is killing me though."

"Oh my God! I am so sorry. I totally forgot about that. I'm such an idiot. Let me take you home." Justin immediately moved more into his seat. He had to adjust the hard on that tented his pants. Quickly buckling his seatbelt, he pulled out of the parking lot and headed to my apartment.

CHAPTER 21

"*J* can walk." I squirmed in Justin's arms.

"You can hobble. I don't want you hurting your ankle more than it already is." Justin stepped from the elevator with me still in his arms.

Mrs. Buchanan decided then was the perfect time to step out of her apartment. "Oh! Did you two get married? I'm a bit hurt you didn't invite me, Justin."

I furrowed my brow. "Mrs. B, we didn't get married. I hurt my ankle, and Justin felt the need to be a caveman."

"Oh, you poor dear! Let me get your parents to open the door for you." Mrs. Buchanan briskly walked over and banged on the door. She kept up the banging until my dad opened the door.

"Mrs. Buchanan, I am not massaging Asshole's asshole again!" My dad yelled at my neighbor before she could say why she was knocking. Mrs. B just pointed toward Justin holding me in his arms.

"Oh, good Lord! What did you do now, Cierra?"

"Thanks, Dad."

Dad moved out of the doorway while Justin carried me over to the couch.

"Jerry, who was at . . . What the hell happened?" Mom dropped the dishtowel she was holding and ran over to the couch.

"I twisted my ankle."

"Is this because of you, boy?" Dad stood facing Justin with his arms crossed.

"Maybe?"

With the look my father was giving Justin, I was happy to know he didn't own a gun. Dad would have shot him on the spot.

"Knock it off, Jerry. Go get the ice pack out of the freezer, grab a couple pain relievers out of the bathroom and get some juice." Dad continued to stare at Justin.

"Jerry. Now!" Mom snapped.

"Fine. You always ruin my fun."

Mom sighed as Dad followed her demands. "Sorry about that, Justin. Her father can be a bit overprotective."

"I can hear you, Margaret."

"I know you can. Your daughter is in pain so hurry up, please." Her sickeningly sweet voice rang through my apartment.

"I will be fine, Mom. My heels just got caught on some loose gravel, and my ankle gave out."

"Sure, honey." Mom turned toward Justin after she placed a pillow under my ankle. "Cierra has always been a little klumsy. It's impossible to count how many injuries she's had by just walking down the street." Mom gingerly touched my ankle. "I'm guessing you found her tonight. Did she finally let you talk to her?"

A crimson blush bloomed on his cheeks. I figured with the look he had on his face I wasn't supposed to know that little nugget of information. Justin was a putz if he thought my mother was going to keep that a secret.

"That's how you knew where I was tonight?" I asked.

"Guilty. I stopped by here about an hour after the decorators left. I missed you by fifteen minutes. Your parents heard me out and took pity upon me."

"Traitors." I ground out through my clenched jaw.

"No, sweetie. I felt bad for the boy. He went to all this trouble to show how much he cares about you. I just gave him the address to where you were going to be. It was up to him to woo you from there."

My mom clearly thought we lived in a Jane Austen novel. Crossing my arms, I glared at the two conspirators.

"Woo me?"

"Clearly he swept you off your feet." My mom burst into giggles. Her giggles became so out of control she slapped her hand on the couch. Unfortunately, it slammed directly on my ankle instead. Pain shot up my leg causing me to bite back a scream that would have had the police knocking on the door.

"Holy Mother-"

"Watch your language young lady! Even if it is your mother's fault for slapping your injured ankle." Dad placed the ice pack gently on my throbbing joint then handed me the pain reliever with a glass of juice. Then as if I wasn't laying in agony on the couch, Dad returned to the recliner and resumed watching a taped hockey game.

"I'm going to go back to the dishes. If you need anything, just yell. Come on, Jerry."

"What? I'm watching the game. The Bombers are up by one."

"NOW!" She yelled from the kitchen. Dad grumbled, pausing the game again then walked toward the kitchen. He mumbled something that sounded like "good thing she's hot."

Ew! I was going to have to bleach my brain.

Justin stood awkwardly in front of the couch. He had his hands shoved in his pockets. I admired him unabashedly. His hair looked like he had run his hands through it one too many times. The coat he still wore was open and showed the green and red rugby shirt he had on underneath. Jeans outlined his muscled thighs with a small rip artistically made near the knee. A pair of leather sneakers topped off his very relaxed look.

"So . . ."

"So."

"The decorator did a great job. It looks wonderful in here." Justin took in the handiwork of his minions.

"Yes, they did."

"Did you like the flowers?"

"Yes, I did."

Justin huffed out a breath and squatted next to the couch. "Can we go back to when we were in the car?"

I snapped my head to look toward the kitchen. My parents were huddled together discussing something.

"We can't with my parents here." I whispered.

He laughed showing me the rare dimple that I've come to love. "I meant when we were talking more than three-word sentences."

"Oh. Ok sure. Let me ask you a question."

"Anything, baby." Justin brushed a strand of hair out of my face. His hand lingered on my cheek caressing it lightly making me shiver.

"Why did you do all this?" I waved my arm around indicating the whole apartment.

"I thought you might want Christmas to be special this year."

"What are you talking about?"

Justin rocked back and sat cross-legged in front of the couch. "I remembered you talking about how your grandmother had recently passed away. You said she was always the one who made Christmas feel special. I wanted to make sure you had that this year."

Tears threatened to spill at the thought of my sweet grandmother. All of a sudden, the back of the couch got really interesting.

Wait! What is that stain? My eyes fell on a white stain on my dark couch.

"Cierra?" Justin gently turned my face back toward him.

A lone tear slid down my cheek. He leaned forward and kissed the track of that lone tear.

"Thank you, Justin." The gravel in my voice let slip the pain I felt.

"I'd do anything to make you happy, Cierra. If only you'd let me."

Our lips met in a soft kiss. The light of the Christmas tree and the soft glow of the twinkle lights swathed throughout the apartment lent a level of romanticism I'd never experienced. I pulled him closer. His chest was pressed against mine while I ran my cold hands underneath his shirt. The muscles in his back tightened and relaxed with ever pass of my fingers.

"Uh hmm. If you two are done, I'd like to finish the game." Dad said shattering the moment.

"Jerry!" Mom rushed over and tried to block Dad from resuming his position in front of the TV.

"Margaret! Clearly, they need a chaperone. They almost had sex on the couch."

"Dad!" I exclaimed.

"Jerry!" Mom snapped at the same time.

Laughing, Justin stretched his body as he unfolded himself from the floor. "I need to go. Can I come by tomorrow? Maybe talk about the ball?"

"Sure." With one last sweet kiss, Justin left shutting the door quietly behind him.

"That man is a keeper." Mom swooned.

I couldn't tell her that I already knew that, and it scared me to death.

"Yeah! A *zoo*keeper if he willingly wants to come into this family."

"Dad!"

"Jerry!"

Dad grinned at us then went back to his hockey game.

CHAPTER 22

"*C*ierra, your two o'clock is here." Janice's voice squawked through the speaker on my desk.

"Please send him in." I shuffled the papers I'd prepared.

"Well, hello gorgeous." Jonas walked in and picked me up in a fierce hug.

I giggled. "Let me go, you big oaf!"

"Ok. Ok." Jonas looked around my office before taking a seat. "Nice digs you have."

"Thanks. It kinda feels like a step up from a closet, but it's my closet."

"It's a nice closet. Especially with those. Did pretty boy send you those?" He pointed to the flowers on my desk.

"You know his name is Justin."

"Of course he did." Justin walked into my office, smirking at Jonas. "How are you doing, Jonas?"

They shook hands and glared at each other.

I rolled my eyes at the overly manly display. "I didn't know you were coming to this meeting."

Justin glanced at me. "I actually came to invite you to lunch. When I talked to Janice, she mentioned you were meeting with Jonas. I thought I'd pop in to say hi and listen to what you have planned so far."

That was such a bullshit answer. He knew exactly what was planned. While I was nursing my ankle, he came over and worked on the plan with me.

Lord save me from jealous men.

"Alright. If everyone will have a seat, I can go over what I have in mind."

For the next hour Jonas, Justin and I ironed out all the details for the ball that would be held at The Grand Hotel. It would have all the glitz and glamour of a movie premiere but with the added twist of people being able to bring their own furry friends. Hors d'oeuvres for both human and furry friends would be served. Jonas also agreed to bring a few of the animals up for adoption.

"Are you sure we can do this in less than two weeks?" Jonas asked.

I swallowed the lump in my throat. "Well, I kind of already booked the room and caterer for December 28th."

Their eyes snapped to me. "How did you know Jonas would agree to everything?"

"I've worked with Jonas long enough to know what he would like."

Justin furrowed his brow and looked at Jonas.

Jonas had a cat who ate the canary look on his handsome face.

"Good girl. I had faith in you that you'd pull this together. I can't wait to see how this ends up," Jonas looked at his watch. "I better get going. Animals need to be fed and walked."

"Thank you for coming, Jonas. I promise we will save your shelter."

Jonas winked. "I know you will."

We all stood. I gave Jonas a quick hug while Justin gave him a sturdy handshake.

"Give my love to Artie and Obie. I will be in touch if I need your approval for anything else."

"No need. Just give me a final date, time and how to dress. I will be there with bells on." Jonas left my office closing the door behind him with another wink.

Justin and I stood staring at the closed door.

"Are you always so presumptuous when it comes to planning?" Justin's voice was flat.

"Of course not. This is a special case. We are short on time and decisions need to be made quickly. On top of that, I have known Jonas going on 10 years. I knew he'd like my ideas and agree with my choices." I narrowed my gaze. "Why are you questioning me about this?"

Justin cleared his throat. "I'm sorry. I was thrown for a loop when you said you'd moved forward without talking to Jonas first."

"I have more work to finish before lunch. You can see yourself out, Mr. Remington." The tension in the air was thick.

I forced myself to sit behind my desk and look at the papers in the file for the ball.

The chair was yanked to the side. Justin caged me into my chair and put his face a few scant inches away from mine.

"I will leave in a minute. I said I was sorry. It was an asshole thing to say. My CEO popped out for a minute."

"Ok."

His hand reached up and caressed my cheek.

"Let's go to lunch today."

"Who are we going to be?"

"What do you mean?" Justin's gaze followed his fingers with each caress of my face.

"Are we going as Cierra and Justin? Or are we going as Mr. Remington and his corporate event planner, Cierra Jameson?"

Justin stopped petting me. His eyes flashed with something I couldn't make out.

"We are always Justin and Cierra. I will never treat you any differently."

"There will come a time when you have to, Justin."

"Come to lunch with me."

My eyes locked with his. For a moment, the world around us stopped. All that existed were the two of us. I finally managed to pull my gaze away from his.

"Alright."

Justin's hand snaked around my neck and pulled me to him. Our lips collided in a rough kiss. The urgency and need I felt from him had electricity shooting to my core. I ran my hands up his muscled chest. My fingers curled into the hair at the nape of his neck. He moaned into my mouth. I had to clench my thighs together aching for relief.

Justin pulled an inch back from my lips. "Good. I will come get you at 1. Be ready."

Closing the space between us, he slowly kissed my lips. He devoured the moan I couldn't hold in any longer. Just as the kiss started to become more, Justin jerked back. He straightened his shirt, tie and jacket. He had a noticeably large bulge in his pants. My hand covered my mouth before a giggle could escape. I did that to him. There was something about having that kind of power over a man like Justin Remington.

CHAPTER 23

$\mathcal{N}$umbers of the descending floors flashed on the screen in the elevator. People crowded around me anxious to get off. I caught my reflection in the stainless steel doors. The butterflies in my stomach took flight at hyperspeed.

Justin's assistant had called only minutes earlier asking I meet him in the lobby. I had completely lost track of time and ended up throwing my jacket and scarf on while striding to the elevator.

A ding announced my destination. The others in the elevator with me flooded out. While they hurried out, I took a deep breath and pulled my confidence over me like a blanket.

The lobby was busy this time of day. Noise of conversations and others walking to and from elevators muffled the click of my heeled boots on the marble floor. Justin chatted with the security guard unaware of my approach.

Tapping him on the shoulder, he spun around holding two bags. "Hi."

His mouth tilted up on one side while his eyes glided over me. "Hey, baby."

Heat flushed my face. "Ready?"

"Definitely." Justin gestured forward for me to start walking.

We walked past a few executives that I remembered from the party. Katrina was among them. She grinned and winked.

Outside I turned to Justin. "Where are we going?"

"It's a surprise. Come on." Justin slid the hand not holding the paper bags into mine tugging me with him.

"No hints?"

The grin he flashed me was all the answer I was going to get.

We walked a block down and turned down a side street. A chill in the air had me thankful I'd remembered my scarf but wishing I'd remembered my gloves. Flurries floated around us. My body was drawn closer and closer to Justin's warmth. His hand squeezed mine.

"Here we are." He pointed to the open expanse in front of us.

"Really?"

A small park with benches, an ice rink and a children's play area bustled with people. Kids squealed and yelled while parents watched from picnic tables. Each table had a large metal umbrella like structure next to them. A small shed with a counter offered skate rental, hot chocolate, hot dogs and first aid.

"Let's eat. I'm starving." Justin pulled me over to one of the empty picnic tables.

"Are we having hot dogs?"

Justin saw that I was looking at the shack. "Nope. How do chips and sandwiches sound?"

"Perfect." I took one of the bags. The aroma of fresh baked bread floated up from the bag.

We ate in silence and watched kids skating. Two kids caught my eye. A little boy about six held the hand of an even younger girl as she tried to skate. The little girl yanked her hand away, and immediately lost her balance falling on her butt. She wailed while the boy threw his hands up in frustration. A woman, presumably their mom, skated up to them picking up the little girl and ushering the boy to the exit.

"They are cute, aren't they?" Justin asked.

"Definitely."

The woman with the children glanced over and saw us staring. She smiled and whispered something in the little boy's ear. He looked up and ran toward our table without taking his ice skates off. Justin opened his arms letting the boy jump into them.

"Uncle Justin!" He squealed.

"Oof! You are getting so big Henry."

"Did you see me? I've been practicing like you told me."

"I did. I also saw you were helping Willa."

The little boy sighed dramatically. "She is such a baby. Mom makes me hold her hand when she wants to skate, but she just pulls away and falls down. She is slowing down my progress."

"Henry, you need to be nice to your little sister. She is smaller than you. Being the big brother you need to always protect her. Got it?" Justin chucked him on the chin.

Henry looked at me across the table. Until then I had been a silent observer. "Who are you?"

"Henry!" The little girl toddled over calling for her brother. "Uncle Ustin." She called after noticing whose lap Henry was sitting on.

Henry continued to stare at me. "I'm Cierra."

"Henry! Willa! Are you two disturbing your uncle's date?" The woman strode over wearing jeans, knee-high snow boots and a puffer jacket. She carried a stuffed gym bag with skating equipment peeking out.

"Hey Honor!" Justin stood letting the little boy slide off his lap. Picking up the pretty woman, he swung her around with Willa squealing to be picked up too.

"Let me down you idiot!" Honor smacked Justin's shoulder.

Justin let her go and turned toward me. "Honor meet Cierra. Cierra, this is my sister, Honor Remington."

"Nice to meet you." I smiled.

"These two are Willa and Henry." Justin ruffled Henry's hair while Willa tried to jump into Justin's arms.

"I finally get to meet the infamous Cierra." I looked at Justin who had a horrified look on his face. "He's been mooning over you for months. I'm glad he finally grew a pair and asked you out."

"Mooning over me huh?"

"Anyway . . . how are you doing, Honor?"

Honor's face became sadder. When she looked at Henry and Willa she pasted on a bright smile. "Henry, can you take Willa over to the swings?"

"Aww, Mom. That's not fair."

"Please Henry. Just for a little bit while I talk to Uncle Justin."

"I can go with them." I volunteered.

Honor looked at me and smiled. "You don't mind?"

"Not at all."

"Henry! Willa! Stay with Uncle Justin's friend, Cierra."

Willa pegged me with her big blue eyes. "Will you push me on the swings?"

"I sure will." Her little hand grabbed mine and immediately started pulling me toward the swings.

For the next half hour, I found myself pushing Willa on swings, watching Henry climb on the monkey bars and went down a very cold metal slide with Willa in my lap. Landing on the cold ground had me understanding why I never played like this anymore.

My work clothes didn't prepare me for the cold and chill of playing with two cute, rambunctious kids. Willa tried making a snow angel with the coating of snow on the ground while Henry ran around attempting to make snowballs. Both were epic fails.

Through their playing I learned quite a lot. Willa wanted a unicorn for Christmas, Henry wasn't sure if Santa was real anymore, their Grammy is sad now that Grampa is in heaven, and Mommy had been crying a lot when she thinks they are in bed.

As I pushed Henry and Willa on the swings, I asked, "Where is your dad?"

"Dad lives with Astrid now. She's nice, but she makes mommy mad," Willa said.

"Oh. Do you get to see him?"

"Sometimes. He's usually too busy though. Astrid is going to have a baby, and Dad said he has to focus on him." Henry stopped swinging and looked at the ground.

"Oh." I was at a loss for words.

"Cierra, can I ask you a question?" He asked looked at the ground.

"Sure."

Sighing, his big brown eyes looked at me. "Do you think I could ask Santa to bring our old daddy back?"

My heart clenched in my chest. "What do you mean?"

"Before Daddy met Astrid, he'd play with us and love us. Now, he doesn't even care." Henry kicked a stone hidden under the thin layer of snow.

"Well, Santa can do a lot of things because he is magic. Maybe you should ask your dad for that instead of Santa."

Henry stared at me for a long moment then said, "Ok."

"Cierra!" Willa yelled. "I want to go higher."

"Willa, stop shouting. Thank you for playing with them." Honor was steps away from where I stood. Her brown eyes were red rimmed.

"No problem. I'd hang out with these two ruffians anytime." I smiled at them.

Willa ran up and hugged my legs. "I'm gonna miss you."

"I'll miss you too, sweetie." I ruffled her snow hat on her head.

Honor looked at me. "You're good for him. Don't let him be an ass."

I nodded and walked toward Justin who was standing next to the table we were at.

"Cierra!"

I turned and saw Henry running toward me. His booted feet slowed him down. I squatted to his level, and he threw his arms around my neck.

"I'm glad you're Uncle Justin's friend. Will you be my friend too?"

I had to swallow before answering. These kids were giving me all the feels today. "Of course, Henry. Are you sure I'm not too old to be your friend?" I teased.

He shook his head. "Nope. You're the best." Giving me one last squeeze, Henry ran back to his mom and sister.

Justin helped me up from my squatting position.

"Well, you have a new fan club." He smirked when we walked over to the trashcan to dispose our lunches.

"What can I say? I'm awesome."

"That you are. Thank you for playing with the kids. I usually come here every Tuesday to have lunch with them and watch them skate while Honor and I talk. She's going through a lot right now."

"Henry told me some of what is going on. I take it that Dad got a girlfriend knocked up and now they are going through a divorce."

"Bingo! I didn't realize the kids knew so much. I'm going to have to tell Honor about it."

"It sounds like her ex is being an ass when it comes to the kids."

"Yeah. All of this came crashing down the weekend before Thanksgiving. Honor didn't even know that he'd been cheating on her. Let alone getting the girl pregnant. He moved out on Thanksgiving while she was over at my parents' house. As you know, my dad passed away that following weekend. So, it has been a real catastrophe the last few months."

I squeezed his hand. "That is horrible. Sounds like she deserves a lot better."

"Definitely. Unfortunately, my life isn't the only one my mother likes to meddle in. Honor married her husband out of loyalty to my parents. It just so happens she also loved him. You can guess whose side she is on. If Honor and Steve divorce, the businesses that were combined with their marriage could lose millions."

I gasped at how Justin talked about it. His gaze landed on my horrified look.

"Oh God!"

Justin stopped and turned toward me. We were standing right outside of the building. "You have to know I don't care about the money we could lose if they got divorced. I would rather have my sister, niece and nephew be happy than stay with someone because of money."

"I can't imagine anything she is going through. My heart breaks for her and the kids."

Justin linked his fingers with mine as we walked into the lobby. "I've kind of made it my mission to make it a great Christmas for the kids."

"Have anything in mind?"

"I've already done all the traditional things with them. I'm at a loss."

"I might have an idea, but let me try to figure things out first."

In the elevator, Justin turned toward me, backing me into the corner.

"What are you doing?" I looked up at the numbers speeding us up to my floor.

"Kissing you." Justin's lips found mine. His hands slid inside my jacket and caressed my waist. Tilting his head, he deepened the kiss and pulled me closer.

A throat clearing shocked me back to reality. Trina held the elevator doors open. My face felt like it was on fire. I slid away from Justin and adjusted my clothes.

"Have a good lunch?" Trina asked as I walked by. Laughter floated toward my now retreating back.

"Wait." Justin caught up with me and put his hand in mine.

We walked past Janice, and she had a grimace on her face. When she glanced at our linked hands her eyes snapped back to her screen. Justin opened my door and escorted me in.

"I'm late for a meeting, but I want you to come over tonight."

"Ok." I said.

"I've got to leave early, but I will have Sam bring you over." Justin brushed my lips with one final kiss.

CHAPTER 24

The giant TV played a particularly gruesome reenactment. I grimaced and looked away from the screen. Rascal huffed with my sudden movement. He laid between Justin and I on the couch. Justin's arm was slung on the back of the couch. His fingers played with my ponytail.

The empty pizza box sat on the coffee table in front of us. An impromptu picnic dinner of pizza and wine had me feeling relaxed. Watching a true crime documentary, having a giant fur ball warming my lap and a sexy man playing with my hair had me happy to die right then.

"How can you watch this?" Justin paused the screen.

"They are addictive. I try to figure out what really happened."

"Yeah and with any gory scenes you turn away."

"Just because I like the mystery doesn't mean I like the blood and gore." I crossed my arms.

Justin had a devious smile on his face. He tapped the back end of Rascal making the dog dramatically move off the couch. Prowling over toward my end of the couch, I scooted back until my back hit the armrest.

"What are you doing?"

"The one thing I've been thinking about doing since I met you." Justin settled himself between my legs.

"What is that?" I attempted to sound sexy, but it sounded more like I had something in my throat.

"This."

His kiss was soft and inviting. He tasted like the red wine we'd had with dinner. A zing of passion shot down my body. With my moan, he took advantage and slid his tongue inside my mouth. My hand ran over his defined chest and over his broad shoulders. His moan gave me goosebumps.

He pulled back with a glazed look in his eyes. "If we don't stop soon, I don't know if I will be able to."

"I didn't say stop." I attempted to pull his mouth back to mine.

Justin took my hands and put them over my head. "Are you sure?"

I stilled. Looking at the sexy man in front of me what other answer could there be? "Of course."

In a flash, Justin jumped off me. He pulled me off the couch and against his hard body. His hands grabbed behind my thighs and picked me up. I quickly wrapped my legs around his waist.

My lips slammed against his while he carried me down the hall to his bedroom. Rascal thought it was a game. Following us he barked and jumped. I started to giggle.

"Rascal! Knock it off. You're ruining the mood." I tucked my face into his shoulder and laughed even harder.

Justin slammed the door behind us. A whining Rascal pawed at the door. Justin threw me on a huge bed. In one bounce, I landed on the edge of the bed and slid off the opposite side.

"Shit!" Justin ran over to me.

I laid on the floor laughing.

"Are you ok?" He bent down and pulled my hands from my face.

"Yes." I sucked in a deep breath trying and failing to pull myself together. Another fit of giggles erupted from me.

"If you are finished, I'd like to get back to what we were doing on the couch."

Smiling wickedly, I said, "Yes, please."

Justin helped me up pushing me gently on the bed.

He began kissing my neck. I laced my fingers through his hair while grinding my hips against his. A need came over me like a wildfire.

"I need you to take your shirt off." My hands reached for his shirt. He pulled back and ripped it off tossing it to the floor.

"Now you." He demanded while batting my hands away from his perfect abs.

I started to rip my shirt off too but realized I needed to unbutton the blouse. Blowing out a frustrated breath, I couldn't get my fingers to operate the buttons correctly.

"Let me help." I watched as his nimble fingers slowly unbuttoned my blouse. The smirk on his face became more and more devilish with every button.

When the last button was loose, he slid the silky material down my shoulders. His strong hands sent goosebumps along my arms with each caress. Instead of taking the blouse completely off, he took my wrists still bound by the cuffs and pulled my arms up.

"What are you doing?"

"Lay back and let me enjoy you." Hooking the blouse around the pointed end of the headboard left me exposed from the waist up.

Justin ran his hands over my bra-covered breasts and down my stomach to the top of my skirt. Those hands reached around and slowly pushed the zipper down.

I took a shuddering breath. Heat sizzled through my veins. Justin continued his slow torture. He finally ripped my skirt off, throwing it into the dark abyss behind him.

Justin sat back on his knees. His gaze felt like a physical caress. My pebbled nipples were begging to be sucked. The thin panties I wore became even more transparent with every second.

"You are so beautiful. In fact, beautiful isn't a good enough word to describe you. Heavenly, immaculate, and pure perfection is more like it." A very unladylike snort escaped when he finished waxing poetically about me.

Justin licked his lips. "I'll make you a believer."

CHAPTER 25

"*I* will be right back." Justin ran from the room.

I took the time to look at my surroundings. The beautiful bed I was laying on had an ornate wooden headboard that I was attached to. Gray walls had minimal decorations. Dark hardwood floors were covered with a single rug with swirls of dark and light colors. I couldn't make out much more since in our hurry neither of us bothered with a light.

"I'm back." The sexiest man I'd ever seen was striding over to me with a small bowl in his hand. I craned my neck but couldn't quite make out what was in there.

"Good because my arms are getting tired." I tried wiggling my arms free but let out a frustrated huff.

"I'm sorry, sweetness, but I want you like this a bit longer."

Justin pulled something out of his pocket. The tie he'd wore earlier dangled from his hand.

"What are you doing now?"

"Up for a little excitement? I promise you will love it. If at any time you don't, let me know, and we will stop."

I looked at the tie and then at Justin. With a nod, he wrapped the tie around my eyes eradicating my view.

"Are you ok?" Justin's disembodied voice brushed over my skin.

I swallowed and nodded.

"Good." He growled.

Anticipation sung through my body. I moved my hips and body urging him to touch me.

Finally, I felt one finger trail from my collar bone to my cleavage. It went into the cup of one breast circling my nipple. My nipple became painfully hard.

Justin pulled down the cup of my bra. A cool breeze floated over my exposed nipple making me shudder.

I heard clinking then a biting cold circled my nipple.

"Holy shit!" I squealed.

"You like that?"

"What was that?"

"Ice cube. Don't worry. I'm going to warm it back up." With that he sucked my nipple into his warm mouth.

A loud moan echoed through the bedroom.

Justin continued his torment on my nipple. Alternating between the cold ice cube and his warm mouth. My panties had to be soaked, and I had a feeling he'd just begun.

While he sucked on the one tortured breast his fingers played inside the cup of the other. Everything felt heightened with my eyes covered. Every slide of his tongue and caress of his hand felt more intense.

"Please Justin." I begged.

"Tell me baby. Tell me what you need." He pinched the still-covered nipple.

"I need you on my other nipple."

"I'm here to serve you." Justin moved to the other breast, freeing it from the cup.

Using the ice cube and his mouth, he brought me to the edge of sanity until I finally toppled over the cliff and fell into the depths of ecstasy.

"Oh God! Justin!" My body shook with a blinding orgasm. He had only been worshiping my breasts and I'd already come. This man might just kill me.

"That was exquisite." He let me ride out the aftershocks of pleasure.

When my body had come down, I felt the ice cube again. Placing it between his teeth, he drew it down my stomach. His warm lips soothed as the ice pebbled my skin.

His fingers hooked into the top of my panties. Pulling them down, he followed behind with the ice cube. There was a pop. The ice met the steamiest part of my body. Justin teased me by dragging the ice over my hip, down my thigh and up the opposite.

I squirmed. My body tensed with the anticipation of that ice cube on my most sensitive part. I took deep breaths but my heart beat erratically in readiness. Finally, he lightly touched the ice to my hard clit.

"Holy fuck!" I screamed.

"You ok?" Justin stopped his ministrations to ask.

"That was a good holy fuck. Keep going or I'm going to kill you."

His deep laugh sent shivers down my body. Making my already wet pussy drenched all over again.

"That would be interesting. Seeing as you are tied up and blindfolded."

"JUSTIN!" I shouted.

A sucking noise had me stilling.

Another pop then a cold tongue laved over my clit.

I moaned obscenely.

"You taste so good. I want you to come on my tongue. Can you do that, baby?"

Before I could answer, Justin sucked my clit into his cool mouth. The swirling of his tongue around my hard nub had me arching my hips into his face.

He moaned into my wet mound. Justin slid one of his thick fingers past my lips and began alternating between pumping and sucking.

Desperate for another release and begging for more, I pumped my pussy on his face and finger. Justin slid another finger in. He bit lightly down on my clit. My back bowed with the pleasure. Stars burst in the darkness of the blindfold.

"Come for me, Cierra." Justin ordered.

"I'm so close. Please make me come."

His flicking tongue, pumping fingers and my rising hips brought me so close. But, when he finally curled his fingers to find my elusive pleasure spot, I screamed his name while riding an even more intense climax.

I must have passed out because the next thing I knew Justin was untying the tie. Then he lifted the blouse off the headboard gently rubbing my shoulders to get the circulation back.

Justin kissed my closed eyes. My cheek. My neck. Finally, the soft kiss he placed on my mouth tasted like me.

"Damn, you are hot." He whispered against my skin.

"We better not be done." I rasped out. My voice must have fled while I was screaming.

"I don't want to wear you out." He nuzzled my neck.

I looked down and saw the bulge in his pants. That was mine. Moving away from Justin, I quickly removed the bra that was now strangling me.

"I want this." I cupped the hard bulge rubbing it through his jeans.

A groan of pain or pleasure escaped him. Now, I had the devilish smile. I pushed Justin back. He laid with his hands linked behind his head. The heated gaze watched as I opened the fly of his jeans.

Reaching into his pants, I found my prize. The hard length pulsed in my hand. I needed his pants off like yesterday. With a yank, I managed to get his jeans off without falling off the bed.

Justin laughed watching while I barely saved myself from the tumble. I blushed but it was soon forgotten when I saw the most beautiful cock I'd ever seen. Any woman will tell you a penis is an ugly organ. It's good for only a couple things. Making women come. Making babies. Making women stupid. Justin's would probably do all three. Good thing I'm already on the pill. Just looking at that thing could make me pregnant.

"Uh. Cierra? You're making me a little self-conscious here."

"Sorry. I've just never seen such a pretty peen."

"Thank you I guess."

My eyes met his when I bowed over his cock licking the bead of precum off the tip. Justin sucked in a sharp breath. Using my tongue, I dragged it from the base to the head. The monster grew even harder when I sucked it in my mouth. It wasn't the longest cock I'd ever seen, but this was the only cock I really wanted in my mouth.

Sucking and licking his hard cock was making my pussy ache to be filled. I took him as far as I could. I still had a gag reflex and that thing wasn't going to go far.

"Cierra! I need you to stop." I ignored his warning.

Justin pulled me off his cock and rolled me on my back. "Hey! I wasn't done."

"Yeah, well I need to be inside you when I come. Next time you can suck me dry."

Fumbling with his nightstand, Justin found a condom. I grabbed it from his hand, ripped it open with my teeth, and rolled it down his length.

With one swift thrust, Justin was seated inside me.

"Oh God, you are tight."

"Move, Justin! I need you pounding me now."

Justin groaned. "I'm apologizing now because I am not going to be able to last long."

With that he pulled out to the tip and slammed back into me. The banging of the headboard was the soundtrack to our pleasure. We each shouted the other's name. We begged for more. We begged for it not to stop. When we finally found our edge, we each dove off into the passion we'd created.

"Cierra!" Justin pumped one final time and stopped while he came.

I had no words. The starbursts behind my closed eyes set my body on fire. For the third time that night, Justin rocked my world with a soul-searing orgasm.

The bed bounced when Justin collapsed next to me. I stared up at the ceiling. This man was dangerous. Between his adoration, loyalty, kindness, and his perfect peen, a girl would be a sitting duck for cupid's arrow.

CHAPTER 26

"Wow!" I laid my head on his damp chest.

"I agree." He ran his fingers through my nest of hair.

"Why did we wait so long?"

"That wasn't me, sweetheart."

I grumbled under my breath while drawing my fingers over the ridges of his abs.

"What was that?"

Focusing all my attention on his hot body, I ignored his question.

His hand trailed down my back. When it landed on my side, he started tickling. Squirming away from him was impossible.

"Tell me what you said."

"No." I wheezed out. Now two hands tickled my sides while he straddled my hips.

"Give?"

Tears streamed down my face from laughing. "Fine."

Justin propped himself over me waiting for my answer.

"I said, we could have been doing this long ago if you'd have grown a pair and asked me out."

"That is true. I regret that I didn't do this sooner." Justin slid down my body and laid on my stomach.

I traced the intricate designs that sleeved his arms. "When did you get these?"

His eyes flashed to mine. "It was my bit of rebellion when I was in college. My parents hated these. They hated it even more when I took Honor with me to get her first tattoo."

Justin kissed my stomach and looked into my eyes.

"Have you ever thought of getting one?" He asked.

"Not really. I'm a wimp when it comes to pain."

"Good to know."

I furrowed my brow. "What do you mean?"

He flashed his sexy smile. It was the smile that made me forget my own name.

His hands ran up and down my sides. The beginning of a glazed look took over his face.

"Wait." I said placing my hands on his.

"What?"

"I wanted to talk to you about an idea I had."

"You've got five minutes. Then you're mine again." He slid up my body and wrapping his arm around my waist pulled me closer.

My blood started to ignite all over again. "Ok. Well, I thought that Honor would want to come with me to girls' night at The Cellar."

Justin leaned up and gave me a strange look. "You want to invite my sister to go out with you and your friends?"

"Yeah. I guarantee we will be terrible influences and possibly get her drunk, but I cross my heart she will get home in one piece."

Justin's face softened as he leaned down to kiss me. "I think that is a wonderful idea."

"My idea doesn't stop there. I thought we could give her a break on Saturday and take the kids to the shelter. Then you can take the kids home with you while she comes out with us."

His face lit with a grin. "You know you are making it hard not to fall for you, Cierra."

Breath caught in my lungs as Justin proceeded to worship my body all over again. Soon all thought left my brain except for the pleasure he was giving me.

JUSTIN TEXTED me Honor's number after our steamy night together. When I called her, there was a lot of silence, a squeal, and some watery conversation. While I was still on the phone, Honor told Willa about going with Justin and I on Saturday. Her squeal was even louder than her mother's.

We picked them up early on Saturday. Honor was still in pajamas and looked like she was headed back to bed. I shored up our plans for later that night while she handed Justin the kids' overnight bags. With very little fanfare, we left and drove to the shelter.

"Oh my God! Puppies, kitties, birdies—"

"More people!" squawked Murray.

"That damn bird." Justin muttered under his breath.

Murray squinted his beady eyes on Justin. "Charlatan!"

"What's a Charlie town, Uncle Ustin?" Willa asked.

I giggled behind my hand. Justin shot me a look.

Before Justin could attempt to explain, Murray was at it again. "Lady doth protest."

"Jonas!" I yelled.

"Well what do we have here?"

Willa ran up to Jonas putting on the brakes inches before running into his legs. "We are here for puppies, kitties, birdies, bunnies, and snakes. My brother loves snakes. Mom won't let us get one. But, Henry," Willa turned and pointed to her brother who was eyeing up Murray, "has a plan."

Jonas looked at me but squatted down next to Willa. "Oh yeah? What is his plan?"

Willa glanced back to where Justin and I were standing. "I can't tell you. But, I can whisper a clue in your ear."

Leaning closer to the little man-eater, Jonas cupped his ear. She proceeded to cup her mouth to spill Henry's secrets.

"Willa! Don't tell him the plan. I told you old people can't know about it."

"But, Henry . . ." Willa whined after already telling Jonas.

"Your secret is safe with me. My name is Jonas. I own this establishment. Are you guys here to help me take care of the animals today?"

"You bet. I just want to cuddle them all." Willa bounced from side to side with pent-up energy.

"Alright guys let's—"

"Let's get it started ha." Murray squawked.

"Murray, knock it off." I fussed at the bird.

"Out damn spot. Out." Taking his beak and cleaning his feathers, Murray pretended that he didn't say anything.

"Sorry, Cierra. I've been listening to a lot of audiobooks in the office. Not to mention one of my ringtones is the Black Eyed Peas."

"Well, at least he isn't cursing. Last thing I need are these two repeating his potty mouth."

"Alright troublemakers. Let's go see the kitties." Justin took Willa's hand leading her into the cat room.

"Cierra?"

"Yes, Henry."

"Do I have to go into the cat room? Can I go into the lizard lounge?"

I nodded. He ran to where the lizards and snakes were housed.

"Justin! Remember the three terrors in there."

"Don't worry I'm ready."

With a skeptical look, I walked to the dog kennels to begin walking the dogs.

CHAPTER 27

"*How* did today go?" Honor asked.

"I think it went well. We all worked pretty hard at the animal shelter. Justin took them back to his place so I could get ready and pick you up."

"I'm glad they were good for you two."

"You may not be thanking me for long."

"Why?"

"Willa wants to adopt three kittens, two dogs and a bunny. Henry wanted a ghecko and a snake."

Honor leaned back in the car's passenger seat. She looked up at the roof.

"I'm not terribly surprised. Maybe they should ask their dad for these things." She looked over at me. The same devilish grin Justin had now graced her face.

I snorted and focused back on the road in front of us.

"What did you do today?"

"Well, I planned on having a spa day, a nap and just vegging out until you picked me up."

"That sounds fantastic."

Honor let out a breathy laugh. "Unfortunately, I couldn't manage to do any of that. Laundry needed to be done. Dishes needed washed. Christmas decorations needed to be hung."

"Honor!" I admonished.

"I know. You don't understand."

"Explain it to me." Slowing into a parking space outside The Cellar, I waited for Honor to explain.

"I've forgotten how to relax. I can't just do those things I wanted to do. All I kept thinking about was everything I could get done without the kids home." I shook my head at her. "I fully intended to do those things when I was done the chores."

We stared out the windshield for a moment. I clapped my hands. "Alright. Tonight, you are not mom. Tonight you are Honor. The sexy, incredibly hot single mom."

Sadness crossed her face.

"I know it's not what you want but embrace it. He betrayed your trust. He left you. Don't feel sorry for yourself or what you've lost. Be the awesome woman I know is in there."

Honor wiped a tear. "You don't even know me."

I winked. "True, but your kids have big mouths. So I know more about you than you think." Her eyes grew big. "Now, let's get our sexy butts in there."

Tonight was a special night at The Cellar. Christmas was a week away. That meant the annual Christmas Carol karaoke night was in full swing. The bar was decked out in cheesy Christmas decorations. Two drink specials written in chalk on a board propped next to the bar had clever holiday themes.

The staff wore ugly Christmas sweaters. I groaned seeing them. It brought back the night of my humiliation.

"What's wrong?" Honor leaned close so I could hear her.

"Nothing. Look, there are Katrina and Dinah. They saved us a table." I dragged Honor through the reveling crowd.

I paused next to the table. Two men sat with Trina and Dinah. One was dressed in a very nice looking suit and had his face plastered to his phone. The other looked barely old enough to drink and was chatting excitedly to Trina.

"Uh. Hey guys!" Three sets of eyes swung to me. Dinah looked irritated and Trina looked uncomfortable.

"About damn time you got here." Dinah said.

"Well, hello beautiful ladies. My name is Derrick, and this is my brother Darren." He stuck his hand out for me to shake. My eye caught movement behind him. Dinah held up a gun finger to her head and pulled the trigger.

"Nice to meet you." I reluctantly shook his hand. He quickly bypassed me and shook Honor's hand.

"This is Honor. Be nice." My gaze pointedly shot to Dinah.

"I can be very nice." Derrick said. Honor held her purse in front of her as if it were a shield.

"Alright cool it, Casanova." Darren had finally looked up from his phone.

Honor stared at him. He smiled and stood. "Please have my seat. I will grab two more chairs. Derrick!"

Darren and Derrick left in search of chairs.

"Ok. Who the hell are they?" I asked.

"They are Donny's brothers. They are in town for Christmas." Trina took a sip of her drink.

"Yeah. Our dear friend, Katrina, offered us to entertain them," Dinah spat. "The suit hasn't unglued himself from his phone the whole time. The other one is like a puppy trying to hump every girl's leg."

Before we could talk anymore, Derrick and Darren came back carrying two chairs. Darren placed his next to Honor, and Derrick sat his close to Trina.

"Thank you ladies for letting us crash your girls' night." Darren said to Honor.

Honor blushed and looked down at her hands.

"Yes. Thank you! This was the best idea my brother had." Derrick slid a hand down Trina's arm.

"Hands to yourself, baby brother." Donny snapped.

"What?" Derrick put his hands up.

"You heard me. Drinks are on the house tonight as a thank you for putting up with these two."

"Thanks, Donny. This is Honor. She is Justin's sister."

"Nice to meet you. If you need anything, let me know. It's a bit crazy tonight." A crashing sound and a high-pitched yelp sounded behind the bar. Donny looked skyward then headed quickly to the bar.

"So Honor, welcome to girls' night and the annual Christmas Carol karaoke." A screeching version of *O Holy Night* interrupted Trina. "As you can see, not everyone is a keeper. But, the more you drink, the better they sound."

"Oh great." Honor said meekly.

"Do you want a drink?" Darren asked Honor.

She nodded, and he jumped up from the table.

"You can get me another and a vodka pineapple for Cierra." Dinah shouted.

I waved my hands. "None for me tonight."

Darren nodded and disappeared into the throng of people.

"Looks like you have a fan." I whispered to Honor.

"Oh God." She moaned.

"What? Why is that a problem?" Dinah asked.

"It's not. It's just my relationship with my ex is complicated."

"Screw it or screw him. Either way they are exes for a reason. Let your freak flag fly." Dinah said, chugging the last of her beer.

Darren reappeared with drinks in hand.

"Thank you." Honor gave him a small smile.

Darren flashed a dimpled grin. "No thanks necessary."

I watched as Honor relaxed little by little while talking with Darren. Trina seemed to be flirting with Derrick, and Dinah had disappeared somewhere. Karaoke was purely background noise until they switched to the DJ.

Darren persuaded Honor to dance. Derrick just dragged Trina to the dance floor. I couldn't hold back my smile as I watched Trina dance awkwardly with Derrick. He looked like he was fighting off a swarm of killer bees.

"Well, those boys move fast." Dinah sat next to me watching the couples.

"It's nice to see. Honor has not had the best luck with men, and Trina has had a crush on Donny for so long I never thought I'd see her smile at another man like that."

"I agree."

My jaw dropped, and I looked at Dinah. "No snarky comment? Who are you and where is my friend?"

Dinah punched me in the arm. "Smart ass."

"What the hell are you drinking?"

Dinah sighed. "Maybe it's just the Christmas season." She shrugged and sat back in her seat.

My purse vibrated in my lap. Digging through the small clutch I found my phone. A light signaling a text message flashed.

Mr. McSexypants: How do you get green and red dye out of dog hair?

Me: What?

Mr. McSexypants: We had a bit of a baking incident.

I giggled. Dinah looked over at me and huffed. "Go ahead and talk to your man. I'm gonna see if I can get into some trouble."

Me: What do you mean incident?

Mr. McSexypants: Uhm . . .

Me: Well . . .

Mr. McSexypants: Willa pushed the mixer on high and ingredients went flying. Now, Rascal looks like Christmas threw up on him.

I tried to imagine the cuddly golden retriever now green and red. I didn't have to try for too long when Justin sent me a picture of Henry, Willa and Rascal with red and green splotches.

Me: Try soap and water.

Mr. McSexypants: Don't you think I've tried that?

Me: Did you?

Mr. McSexypants: So, having fun?

Me: Nice diversion. Yes.

Mr. McSexypants: Hope you aren't having too much fun without me.

Me: Hmmm

Mr. McSexypants: I will come down to a bar with these red and green monsters if I have to.

He was so sexy when he got all protective and jealous.

Me: Don't worry. I am sober and relegated to watching couples bump and grind.

Mr. McSexypants: Where's Honor?

Me: She's dancing.

I wasn't sure how much to tell him. So being vague was my best bet.

Mr. McSexypants: Really? By herself?

Me: Uhm

Mr. McSexypants: Tell me

Me: She is one of the couples I'm watching

Mr. McSexypants: WHAT?!

Me: It's harmless. She's smiling and laughing. I think she needed this boost.

Mr. McSexypants: Yeah she did. Thank you for thinking of her.

Me: I like her.

Mr. McSexypants: Sorry you're relegated to watching.

Me: It's ok. I miss you though.

I pressed send then re-read what I wrote.

Oh crap!

My heart started pounding fast. Sweat broke out on my brow. I kept looking at my phone and all I saw were dots signaling he was typing.

How could I be such an idiot?

What if he doesn't have feelings for me after all?

Work would be horrible now.

I was about to throw my phone back into my clutch when it vibrated with a message.

Mr. McSexypants: I miss you too. I miss you all the time. Every moment we aren't together I'm thinking about you. I wonder what you are up to. Are you having a good day? Or night? It takes all of my control not to take the elevator down to your office every day. I more than miss you.

I stared at that message for so long my phone went inactive in my hand. Words evaded me. What could I possibly say back to that?

"Where is everyone?" Donny asked grabbing the empty glasses and bottles.

"Out there." I pointed toward the dance floor.

"Wha-" Donny made a choking noise.

"What's wrong, Donny?" He just stared out at the floor. His face started to become red.

Glancing toward the groups of dancers, I saw Honor dancing close to Darren. Her head propped on his should while he held her. Scanning the other dancers, I almost missed it. Derrick was still dancing with Trina. Only that wasn't what had Donny choking. They were locked in a tight embrace and kissing quite passionately.

"Oh." I said.

"I told him to keep his damn hands to himself." Donny sputtered.

"Why does it matter, Donny?"

"Trina deserves better. She's sweet, kind, beautiful and utterly breathtaking. Derrick won't treat her that way."

Placing my hand on his arm, I said, "I agree, but why do you care? I thought it was Dinah you liked?"

"What?" Donny looked down at me confused.

"You know, Dinah."

Donny looked at me then back to the dance floor. His face became red all over again. Charging onto the crowded dance floor, he tapped Derrick's shoulder. Derrick looked over his shoulder and shrugged then moved back to kiss Trina again. Donny pulled Derrick off of Trina and dragged him outside.

"What is happening?" Dinah plopped back into the chair next to me.

"Looks like Donny finally sees her."

"About damn time." Dinah took a sip of her beer.

Darren walked Honor back to the table, excused himself and followed his brothers outside. Trina found her way back to our table. Tears streamed down her face.

"Why did he do that?"

Dinah and I looked at her then at each other.

"Well?"

"I think that is a question for Donny." I said.

"I just want to go." Trina picked up her purse and turned to leave.

The three men were walking back into the bar. Donny was holding his hand. Derrick prodded his cheek tenderly. Darren had a smirk on his face and just kept shaking his head.

"What the hell was that for, Donny?" Trina pushed Donny's chest.

"Uhm . . . I was just protecting you. Derrick doesn't do

relationships. He uses women and then dumps them. You deserve better."

"Oh yeah? How do you know what I deserve? Who are you to make decisions for me?"

"Uh," Donny sputtered.

"You know what mind your own fucking business, Donny. Come on, Derrick."

Derrick walked over to Trina. Trina tenderly examined his cheek. With a smirk at Donny, Derrick threw his arm around Trina.

"Wait! Where are you going?" Donny asked.

"Back to my place. I'm going to let Derrick fuck my brains out." Trina spat.

Donny stood slack-jawed watching the two of them walk out the door.

"Wow! You guys really know how to throw a girls' night." Honor said.

My phone vibrated on the table.

Mr. McSexypants: Oh God! We have had a glitter explosion. Who packs glitter to stay overnight? It's everywhere. I think its even in my mouth.

I giggled and put my phone back into my purse.

CHAPTER 28

"*I* can't believe I missed all that drama last night." Dean said.

Two Beans and a Latte was typically slow on Sundays. I sat at a corner table with my laptop, my second mochaccino and a banana nut muffin. Dean took a break and settled in the seat across from me.

"It was a hell of a lot of drama. I've never seen Trina like that. She was pissed. Not only pissed but pissed at Donny. I never thought that would happen."

"You miss all the good stuff, big brother. Especially when you have those lame dinner parties."

"Knock it off, Dinah." Dinah sat next to Dean.

She grinned at her brother then took a bite of her cherry danish.

"It was definitely a memorable night."

The bell over the door chimed. Justin strode in looking a little worse than normal.

"Oh man! What happened to him?" Sean asked standing next to the table.

"I would guess it was the six and the three-year-old he had over last night."

After ordering his large coffee, Justin walked over to the table and sat next to me.

"Remind me never to agree to your ideas again." He kissed my cheek.

"It couldn't have been that bad."

His tired eyes looked at me then to our audience. "They didn't sleep last night. How could they not be tired? Between the food coloring and glitter explosions, bath time twice, coloring time and reading time, I was exhausted. They just seemed to get more and more energy."

Everyone looked at the bedraggled man. Laughter rang out around the table. I was laughing so hard, my eyes watered.

"What?" He said swinging his arms up again.

The laughter only increased. Every patron in Two Beans was now staring at us.

"Come on." He whined.

I took a breath to calm my laughter. "Every time you wave your arms, glitter is flying all over. It's like you're a fairy princess."

The appalled look on Justin's face caused everyone at the table to begin laughing.

"I'm never watching those little demons again." He huffed making sure not to move his arms again.

Leaning toward Justin, I whispered in his ear. "I bet if I ask really nicely you will."

His eyes flared with his sexy smile. Even with sprinkles of glitter on his face that smile sent shivers through my body.

"Oh good! They finally did it." Dinah proclaimed loudly.

"What?"

"You two finally had sex . . . the horizontal mambo . . . the beast with two backs . . . fucked . . . made love . . . I could go on."

"Please don't." Justin begged.

"So, was it good?" Dinah asked in a stage whisper. Dean and Sean leaned in to hear my response.

My face flamed, and I looked over to Justin.

"Go ahead. Tell them how godlike I am in bed."

Shoving the muscled man next to me did nothing.

"I am not sharing intimate details of our time together with you gossip hounds."

Dinah winked. "Gotcha! I will call you later."

Dinah walked toward the door, but then she rushed back to her seat. We stared at her odd behavior. With an evil grin on her face, she looked like she was crazy. Well, crazier than normal.

"Just act natural." Of course, we all looked to the door. Trina and Derrick walked in looking a little worn out.

Well, my best friend got some last night.

Lucky bitch!

Our entire table watched them walk over to the counter and place their order. We watched them wait for their order in awkward silence. They were oblivious to us cataloging every move they made. Trina turned to get a table then stopped mid-stride and paled when she saw they were being watched.

I waved them over.

Derrick placed his hand on her lower back, guiding her toward our table.

"Hi guys!" I said a little too cheerily.

"Hey. Uh for those who don't know this is Derrick, Donny's little brother."

"We know." Dean whispered. "Good for you girl."

Trina blushed and looked at the coffee in her hand.

"So, uhm, how are you two today?" I asked.

"Fine." Trian and Derrick said at the same time.

This was weird. There was definitely more to this next day awkwardness.

"Well, we better go. It was good seeing all of you." Trina dragged Derrick out the door.

They all watched as Trina practically dragged Derrick out the door. A few minutes dragged by as they all continued to stare at the door.

"That was fucking weird." Justin said breaking the silence.

"Yeah. There is more there." I nodded.

"Ok. I'm actually going to leave now. We'll see you later tonight?" Dinah asked.

"Oh crap! I totally forgot about tonight. Glad you said something. I will see you guys tonight."

"Ok. Later." Dinah began walkimg back toward her bakery.

"What's tonight?" Justin asked.

"We exchange gifts and eat Chinese the Sunday before Christmas. Things have been so hectic, I completely forgot."

"That sounds fun," he said. "I guess I won't be seeing you tonight then."

I gave him a sad smile.

"Ok."

CHAPTER 29

*T*hree days before Christmas I was busy putting the finishing touches on the upcoming gala. Invitations had gone out the previous week. Having received wonderful feedback about attendance I felt this was truly coming together. However, our booked caterer backed out at the last-minute citing illness and the media company we were working with double booked and canceled our event stating it wasn't high profile enough.

Now, I was frantically begging for replacements. I was so focused on the computer in front of me, I didn't see the person enter my office until the door clicked shut.

Justin loosened his tie and sat in the chair in front of my desk.

"Hello, beautiful."

"Hey Justin. Do you need something? I'm scrambling to rebook a caterer and media relations. Without them, this could crumble around us."

"Look at the time, Cierra."

I blinked then squinted at the clock. 7 o'clock.

"Well, crap."

"Yep. Let me take you to dinner."

"I really need to finish this."

"It can wait until tomorrow. I want to spend some alone time with my girlfriend." That sent a little thrill through me.

A yawn escaped. I saved my work and shut the laptop. "Alright."

Justin grabbed my coat and held it open for me. We held hands through the office to the elevator. Just being together lifted the weight off my shoulders.

We walked through the quiet lobby to through the front doors. I pulled my coat tighter when the cold air blasted us. Snow was falling around us, instantly quieting the city.

"Where are we going?" I asked.

"Not far."

Justin led me to the small Italian restaurant across from the building. Warmth flooded outside when we opened the door. Garlic and spices assaulted my senses. My stomach decided to voice its opinion at that moment.

"Sounds like this was a good choice." My hands covered my stomach as I turned red.

"Guess I was hungry and didn't even know it."

A plump Italian woman walked over carrying water glasses.

"Hello, Signore Justin. How are you tonight?" She kissed him on both cheeks.

"Maria, my love, I've missed you."

She smacked him. "You know my Gustave will take a spatula to you. Now, who did you bring tonight?"

"This is Cierra, my girlfriend."

"A girlfriend! Finally!" Maria made the sign of the cross and folded her hands in prayer.

"Nice to meet you, Maria." I said

"Gustave! Signore Justin finally has a girlfriend."

"Good, he can stop hitting on you now." A muffled voice yelled from the kitchen.

Justin and I laughed.

"I will bring you the best we have." Maria hurried off.

"Been here before?" I asked.

"A few times." Justin smiled. "When I was little, my dad would bring me here for lunch or dinner. He was his best when he talked with Gustave and Maria. I never saw him as relaxed."

Sadness flashed over Justin's face. I reached across the table and gave his hand a squeeze.

"I'm sorry, Justin."

"It's fine. It hit me today that this is the first Christmas without my dad."

"I know how you feel. My gram keeps popping in my head at the strangest times."

"Well, I wanted to ask you something."

"Ok." I said.

"Will you come to my family's Christmas Eve dinner?"

I stiffened. Just thinking of interacting his mother had my stomach turning sour. "Are you sure you want me there?"

"Of course. Why wouldn't I?" He saw the look on my face and added, "Honor and the kids will be there, too. Come save me from the glitter."

I laughed. "I suppose I could go. Unfortunately, I won't be able to stay too long. I have to drive up to my parents that night."

"I understand. I could go with you if you want."

"To my parents? For Christmas?"

"Well, yeah."

I hadn't even thought about inviting Justin to come along. I'd assumed he would be busy with his own family.

"If you want to, I would love for you to come."

"Good."

Maria came back with multiple dishes filled with pasta, sauces, and meats galore. My mouth watered looking at the choices.

Quiet settled between us while we dug in. The explosion of flavors had me moaning. After a particularly good bite I looked at Justin. His fork was poised at his mouth, and he was staring at me.

"What?" I asked wiping the sauce that had dripped on my chin.

Justin's throat bobbed. "That is just so sexy."

"Sauce on my chin?"

"No. Your moaning. I'm just jealous that it's the food making you make that sound."

Heat flashed through me. "It's not like you haven't done that to me."

Justin set his fork on his plate and bit his lip. "I have plans to do it again."

"Yes, please." I said taking a sip of my wine.

Electricity sizzled between us. We continued to stare at each other for a long time. Maria stopped by the table and retrieved the empty dishes. Her smile told us she knew exactly what was happening.

"Maria, we will need the check please."

"No need. It is on the house tonight." She smirked at our smoldering gazes.

"You don't have to do that." Justin protested.

"We are happy you have found someone. Now, you two go have fun." She winked and escaped back into the kitchen.

Justin threw money on the table and grabbed my hand yanking me out of my seat.

"Where are we going?" I asked.

"Your apartment is closer."

CHAPTER 30

The snow had continued to fall while we were having dinner. Justin navigated the streets with as much caution as he could muster. Sexual tension in the car was palpable. My panties were so damp I thought I'd leave a wet spot on the seat.

When we arrived, Justin helped me out of the car. Just as quickly he had my back pressed to the car door. His hard body molded to mine while he kissed me hard. Snow fell around us. Flakes melted on our warm skin. Our kisses became more frantic. I needed him and not against a cold car.

"Let's go." Grabbing his hand, I dragged him toward my building.

Every few feet we would stop and kiss. A 30 second trip to my floor took 20 minutes with our passionate stops. The final one had us banging against the wall next to Mrs. Buchanan's door.

"Cierra?" She peeked out into the hall.

"Sorry, Mrs. B." I said breathless from Justin kissing my neck

"Oh!" Her shocked expression would have made me laugh if Justin wasn't nibbling on my ear making me forget my name.

She smiled and silently closed the door. I thought I heard her mumble something about her needing batteries, but Justin pulled me to my door. His hands continued to wander my body while I tried to focus enough to get my key in the door.

The door opened, and Justin swept me into his arms. His lips crashed down on mine. I held his face to mine.

Ripping his lips from mine, he asked, "Bedroom?"

"Down the hall. Second door on the left." His lips claimed mine again.

In moments, I was laying in the middle of my bed. Clothes littered the floor.

Justin crawled on top of my heated body. Every touch had my blood singing for more. I needed this man more than I'd ever needed anyone.

"I need to be inside you," he panted. The muscles in his arms bulged with the restraint he was using.

"Good. I need you inside me."

I pulled him down to my lips the same time he slammed into me. Our moans echoed off the walls. Each thrust shook the bed, bringing me closer to my climax.

Swiveling my hips, I could feel him hitting that magic spot. Pleasure shot through my veins. My back bowed off the bed. I clenched my walls around his cock making him shutter.

"Cierra! I'm so damn close. Tell me you are there with me." He pounded each word into me.

"YES!" I screamed.

A low moan from him. His entire body went rigid as I felt him shooting inside me. Warmth cascaded over me. Justin's face had a mask of bliss. Those bulging muscles finally gave out, and he laid on top of me. Our sweat-covered bodies were still connected. I could feel his cock softening inside me.

I watched his chest rise and fall. His eyes fluttered closed. A realization washed over me. If he left me tomorrow, I'd be devastated.

I loved this man.

While I waited for the panic to seize me, Justin raised his head off my chest.

"I love you."

Panic and fear raced through me.

Sliding off the bed, I grabbed my robe. "I need to take a shower."

Hurt flashed across his face.

It felt like a red-hot poker was shoved into my chest. Forcing my eyes away from him, I walked to my bathroom and turned the shower on.

"You hid in your bathroom?" Trina asked.

"Yes. I panicked."

"You really are the dumb one, aren't you." Dinah took a bite of her sandwich.

"Oh please. Like you would just lay your heart out like that." I took a bite of my pickle.

"No, I wouldn't, but I haven't been in that situation."

"Do you love him?" Trina sipped her water.

Trina and Dinah stared at me. I knew I loved him. I'd been avoiding him since that night. He emailed asking to have lunch today. To avoid him at all costs, I begged these two to have lunch. Now, I stared at the two people I could tell anything to.

"Yes."

Dinah and Trina looked at one another.

"So, what is the problem? You know he loves you. That's the scary part." Dinah crunched on a chip.

"He told me he loved me right after."

"After what?"

"Come on, Trina. After he fucked her, he let the words drop."

Trina's eyes got wide. "Oh."

All of a sudden, a cold finger of fear slid down my spine.

"What's wrong? You got pale."

I felt like I was going to get sick.

"Dinah! Do something."

"What the hell do you want me to do? I'm a baker not a paramedic." Dinah reached for Trina's water.

"Don't!" Trina yelled.

"We forgot to use something." I swallowed the lump in my throat.

Dinah dropped Trina's water on the table.

"Oh shit."

"Has this happened before?" Trina asked.

"No. The first time we used a condom. We were just really worked up this time."

"You're on the pill, aren't you." Dinah asked with a bit of panic.

"Yes, but I'm not consistent in taking it because it has been a long time since I've had a real boyfriend."

"Should we go make a trip to the pharmacy?" Trina asked.

"She wouldn't know this soon, idiot."

"Hey!"

"Alright you two aren't helping right now. I need to get back. Are you coming with me, Trina?"

She nodded. Grabbing my purse and jacket, I scooped up my trash to throw away. As I approached the trash can, the door to the café swung open. Justin was framed in the doorway. His gaze connected with mine.

I stood frozen. An unreadibly look crossed his face.

"Ms. Jameson, I'd like to meet with you this afternoon."

"I will have to check my schedule, Mr-"

"Make it happen." He walked back out the door.

"Well, shit." I said.

"Wish I could be a fly on that wall." Dinah said to Trina.

The three of us walked out into the cold December day. Flurries floated in the air around us. We bid our goodbyes to Dinah. Trina and I walked the block and a half back to the office.

We didn't talk for the entire elevator ride. Thoughts swirled through my head. This was going to be a terribly awkward meeting. When the elevator stopped at my floor, I moved to exit.

"Good luck." Trina gave me a thumbs-up.

Striding up to Janice, I waited until she was off the phone.

"How can I help you, Ms. Jameson?" Her tone indicated she'd rather do anything other than help me.

"Mr. Remington asked for a meeting this afternoon. Please schedule it with his assistant." My tone brooked no argument from her.

"Yes ma'am."

Walking into my office, I shut the door behind me. I knew how my day was going to end, and it wasn't going to be happily ever after.

CHAPTER 31

ive p.m. came and went without a meeting. Apparently, I wasn't the one with the busy schedule. Tomorrow was Christmas Eve, and I planned to work from home. I wasn't sure if I was still going to Justin's family's dinner.

A ding sounded from the laptop. It was an email from Justin.

To: cierra.jameson@wtrinvest.com

From: jremington@wtrinvest.com

Ms. Jameson,

Sam will pick you up tomorrow at 3 p.m.

—J. Remington

P.S. We will be talking. Be ready.

Blood pounded in my ears. I slammed the laptop shut. Shoving it in my bag, I stormed out of my office. Janice was still at her desk.

I placed a small wrapped gift and card on her desk. "Merry Christmas, Janice."

Striding over to the elevator, I heard a gasp from behind me. A small smile touched my lips.

SAM PULLED up to my building at exactly 3 p.m. I finished packing my bag while I waited for the knock. When I didn't hear the knock after ten minutes, I opened my door. Sam was standing in front of Mrs. B's door holding a yowling Asshole.

"Just hold him still while I put his drops in." Mrs. Buchanan held a bottle in her hand.

"Ma'am I really need to go." Sam protested while still holding the horrible creature.

A giggle escaped. Two sets of eyes turned toward me.

"Mrs. B., did you hijack my ride?" Leaning in my doorway, I enjoyed the sight before me.

"I needed a strong man's help. It just so happened he walked by when I needed someone. Now, be still, Asshole."

"What?" Sam looked at me for an explanation.

"It's the cat's name." I picked up my bag and shut my door. "Are we going, Sam?"

He widened his eyes and looked at the thrashing cat.

I took Asshole from him. The cat immediately calmed and rubbed against me. I thrust him into Mrs. Buchanan's arms.

"Have a good night, Mrs. B."

Mrs. Buchanan's hand shot out and grabbed my jacket. "What happened to that sexy boy you had? If you ask me, you are trading down now."

"He is just my ride. I'm going to be meeting Justin."

Mrs. Buchanan relaxed. "Oh good. Let me tell you something, Cierra. After seeing the two of you the other night. WhooWe! That was some sexy action. I had to break out new batteries."

"Well, thanks, Mrs. B. Have a great Christmas!" I moved as quickly as possible to the elevator.

"You too, dear."

Sam and I rode the elevator to the lobby. Exiting he asked, "Was she talking about what I think she is talking about?"

My body convulsed with a shudder. "Just don't think about it."

He nodded and opened the car door for me. Before he shut the door, he said quietly, "I will need to bleach my brain."

Sam drove us through the city. A light snow fell as the car

soundless passed holiday revelers. Exiting the city, a peaceful calm fell with the snow. The houses became more and more extravagant. No more fun silly decorations. The mansions had elegant decorations. Not one had wild colors or inflatable lawn ornaments.

What Christmas must have been like for Justin. Growing up around such opulence and luxury. Nothing fun or silly allowed. Would I ever been accepted in a world like this? I am far from proper or rich. I'd be more at home with the help than with the owners of these homes.

Sam pulled up to a beautiful mansion. No lights decorated the home. No wreaths or candles. If I didn't already know it was Christmas Eve, this house would have me wandering if it was happening at all.

The car door opened. Sam stood stiffly and refused to look at me. Darkness shrouded the front of the house. With a steadying breath, I walked toward the door.

"Ms. Jameson, you may leave your bag here." Sam nodded toward the duffle bag in my hand.

I tossed the bag in the backseat.

There was movement in the window. Curtains fluttered before a light turned on illuminating the steps. The stone steps were slick from the falling snow. My booted foot slipped, and I flailed hoping to grab onto the handrail.

There was no handrail.

A loud thwap sounded when my back hit the bottom step. Air whooshed out from my lungs. Stars were in my eyes and my vision began blackening around the edges. I fought to stay conscious. I could hear Sam's footsteps and another person shouting near where I lay prone on the ground.

"Cierra! Oh my God!" Honor rushed down the few steps

"Ms. Jameson, are you alright?" Sam kneeled by me.

All I could do was nod.

I was laying flat on my back in front of my boyfriend's mom's house. A mom that already doesn't like me.

Way to go.

Honor and Sam helped me stand. The world started to spin and I felt myself sway. Nausea roiled in my stomach forcing me to push it down.

Honor and Sam supported me while they rushed me inside to a couch.

"Cierra?" A little voice came from my right.

"I'm ok, Willa. I just had a little accident."

"What is going on?" Justin's voice cut through all the chattering.

"Cierra slipped on the steps coming up to the door. It looks like she took one hell of a fall."

"Oh my God! Baby, are you ok?"

I gave a weak smile.

"I'm going to get some ice. I think she hit her head." Honor left the room.

"Cierra, do you need help?" Henry's voice drew my attention.

"I'll be ok. Thank you, sweetie." I ruffled his hair.

"Can I have a moment with Cierra please?" Justin took the ice pack from Honor. Honor smiled and ushered the kids into the other room.

"Hi." I said.

Justin placed the ice pack on the back of my head. "Hello."

"I really know how to make an entrance, huh." A laugh escaped but was soon followed by a grimace when pain split my skull.

"I know you didn't want to talk to me about the other night, but this is a little extreme." He smiled pushing a loose strand of hair behind my ear.

"Well, that's me, extreme to the max."

Justin groaned at my joke. His forehead met mine. Silence enveloped us. The peace we had in that moment was the most I'd had since we'd last been together.

"Justin! What in the world is going on? Why is that girl here? Why is she sprawled on the couch like a common whore?" Vivienne Remington's voice sliced through our peace.

CHAPTER 32

"*Mother!* I told you Cierra was coming tonight. She is sitting here because you didn't have anyone salt the steps. You're lucky she doesn't sue you."

"I always have to do all the work for you and your sister." The doorbell rang. A rush of cool air flooded into where we were.

Justin looked toward the door. Fury flashed over his face. "You have got to be fucking kidding me."

"What?" I turned to look.

"I promise you I didn't know this was going to happen."

"Am I hallucinating right now? Did I hit my head harder than I thought?" Sicora Reynolds stood in the hallway taking off a fur coat.

Henry and Willa squealed. They ran to a man standing next to Sicora. He stopped them with a hand and patted them on the head.

"Is that Honor's husband?"

"Yep."

"When your mom wants something, nothing stops her."

"Yep."

"Are you sure I'm not hallucinating right now?" I touched my head gingerly.

"Unfortunately, you are not. Want to escape now and head to your parents?" Justin looked at me sincerely.

I was so tempted to say yes. Sitting around a dinner table with Vivienne Remington and Sicora Reynolds sounded like a special kind of hell.

Willa and Henry had sad looks on their cherubic faces. Honor and her husband were arguing not far from them.

This didn't feel like Christmas.

I needed to fix this for them.

"We need to stay. For them." I pointed toward the two sad babes.

He nodded.

"Justin!" His mother called. "Why don't you leave her over there and come entertain your guest."

"Sicora is your guest, Mother. I didn't invite her."

"You should have. She is your fiancée after all."

Sicora sashayed over to Justin. "Hello, baby. I can't believe you forgot to invite me."

Justin grabbed her by the arm and led her toward the door. "What are you doing? You know we aren't together. We are not engaged. I am with Cierra. You need to go home now."

Sicora's bottom lip jutted out. "Don't make me leave. I don't have anywhere to go tonight. Mother and Father are in Europe for the holidays. Let me stay. I promise I will be on my best behavior."

Justin sighed and looked over at me. "Fine. Stay away from Cierra."

"I will. Cross my heart." Her fingers trailed down her obviously altered bosom making a cross.

"Can you believe this shit?" Honor flopped down beside me.

"Uh . . ."

"My mother is fucking unbelievable. I don't know what she thinks she's doing. Steve left me. He has a pregnant girlfriend."

"So why is he here?" I asked.

"He wouldn't say. The only thing he kept saying was he made a mistake. I think my mom offered him money."

"That sucks."

"You got that right. Now, my poor kids don't know what's going on. They barely know it's Christmas. Just look at this tomb of a house we are in. This was not my ideal Christmas for them."

"I agree. This is pretty dreary."

"What are you two plotting?" Justin picked me up, sat down with me on his lap.

"What are you doing?" I tried to squirm away, but he held me tight.

"I like you with her." Honor said.

"Don't change the subject, Sis. What's going on?"

Honor huffed in frustration. "Mom"

"Yeah. Mom."

Before they could get into anything else, we were called for dinner. Justin linked my arm with his. This was a good thing when the world started to spin. He held on to me tightly. We took seats nearest the door for a quick exit if necessary.

"I took the liberty of assigning everyone's seats." His mother pointed out.

All of the adults had name cards on their plates. The children were at a small table inside the kitchen. After going around the table, I didn't see my name.

"Mother, where did you seat Cierra?" His mother took a sip of her wine and shrugged.

"Cierra!" Willa ran up to me. "Your name is with us. We are going to have so much fun. There are chicken nuggets and mac and cheese. If we eat all of our dinner, we can have ice cream."

A tight smile crossed my face as Willa tried to drag me with her. "I'll be right there, sweetheart."

"Ok. Hurry up though, Henry and me are hungry."

I watched the little girl go through the door to the kitchen. "Guess my seat is that way."

A lump grew in my throat. I would not cry in front of these people. His mother would not know how much she hurt me.

"Are you fucking with me right now?" Justin marched into the kitchen while I was frozen in the dining room.

"What's going on?" Honor stood from her seat with her ex and walked to where I was standing.

Justin was a thundercloud when he came from the kitchen.

I touched his arm. "It's not worth it." I whispered into his ear.

Justin looked to Honor. "Did you know about this?"

"What are you talking about?" she asked.

"Cierra is seated in the kitchen with the kids."

Honor snapped her head toward her mother. "No. I didn't know about that."

"Look, it's fine. I don't mind eating with the kids. I think it would feel special for them. If it makes their Christmas better, I am fine eating nuggets and mac and cheese."

Walking on unsteady legs to the kitchen, Willa and Henry cheered when I came in.

I rubbed my hands together. "Now, what are we having again?"

The kitchen door swung open. Justin and Honor strode in carrying chairs.

"What are you two doing?" I asked.

"We wanted to join the fun party. Is that ok?" Justin looked at me then to Willa and Henry.

"Well, I don't know." I looked at Willa and Henry. "What do you think? Should we let them join our special Christmas Eve dinner party?"

"YAY!" Willa yelled.

Henry tried to hold back a smile, but the excitement in his eyes said all that needed to be said.

"Alright, bring on the nuggets and mac and cheese." The cook looked at everyone at the "kiddie" table and smiled. He retrieved another box of mac and cheese. He had to feed more than just the two kids now.

"Isn't your mom going to be upset?" I asked.

"Those people out there she invited. She can have her uncomfortable dinner with them." Justin leaned toward me and kissed me.

"Ew!" came from Henry. Willa covered her mouth and giggled.

CHAPTER 33

*D*inner at the kids' table had never been so fun. When I was a child, I was relegated to the kids' table when all I wanted to do was be old enough to sit at the big table. If anyone had told me I'd be glad to sit at a kids' table at my boyfriend's mother's home, I would have said they were crazy.

Honor, Justin and I delighted in the company of Willa and Henry. Henry shared stories of his classmates, the carol sing-along they did at school and the top-secret project they worked on that his mom wasn't supposed to know about. Willa chattered on about the kids in her daycare and what she wanted for Christmas.

"Cierra, do you think Santa will know where we are if we spend the night here at grandmother's?" Willa asked.

"Of course he can. Don't be stupid, Willa." Henry shook his head at her.

"Henry!" Honor scolded.

"Now, Henry you should be nice to your little sister. She doesn't know everything you do. Plus, Santa is definitely watching you tonight." I said.

Henry pouted then just as suddenly got a devious look in his eye. "Santa can't possibly be watching me. We learned in school there are time zones. If Santa is out delivering right now, there is no way he'd know if I were bad."

He crossed his arms in a "take that" look.

"Time zones don't matter. The elves just call the sleigh and tell Santa there was a change of plans." I clapped my hands together. "Boom! Henry Smithfield doesn't get presents this year."

Justin and Honor snorted. Trying to cover it up with a cough made Justin choke on his own spit.

"I guess you're right. I'm sorry, Willa." Henry hugged his sister.

"May I go up to my room, now?" he asked.

Honor nodded.

As he left the kitchen, we heard, "Santa should have no problem delivering Obie and Alfie tonight."

Justin and I looked over to Honor. Her face paled.

"May I go and watch the Christmas movie?" Willa asked.

"Yes you may."

"Which Christmas movie is she watching?" I asked.

"*National Lampoon's Christmas Vacation*. She thinks it's hilarious. She even quoted it at daycare the other day."

We winced.

"Yep it was that bad. She quoted, "You couldn't hear a dump truck driving through a nitroglycerin plant.""

I snorted out a laugh. "There are worse quotes than that."

"Yes, but whenever her teacher asks what is that sound or asks someone to speak up because she couldn't hear them, Willa breaks out that quote."

Honor, Justin and I cackled. The chef even had a few chuckles.

When we all quieted down, I asked, "How awkward do you think the dinner out there is?"

"Actually, they probably enjoy being their stuffy selves." Honor helped carry the plates to the sink.

A devilish grin curved my face. "Since the children are gone, I have a question for you, Honor."

Honor paused with a plate in her hand. "Ok."

"Hear from Darren?"

A red flush rose from her neck all the way to her hairline. "Who?"

Justin looked between the two of us like he was watching a tennis match.

A blank look crossed my face.

Honor huffed. Setting the dishes back on the table she sat in Henry's seat. "No. I wouldn't expect to hear from him."

"Why?" I asked.

Her eyes darted around the room. "I gave him a fake number."

"Oh my God! He was so into you. Why would you do that?" I sat next to her.

"Who is this guy?" Justin furrowed his brow.

I patted his hand and continued looking at Honor for her answer.

"I know. He was one of the nicest guys I've ever met. I'm not ready for anything new. The kids are still hoping Steve will come back. How could I bring someone new into their lives?" she shrugged.

"Honor, you deserve happiness. The kids will adapt. You need to be honest with them." I squeezed her hand.

"Yes, tell them what a whore their mother is." A venomous voice sounded from the doorway.

"Steve!" Honor jumped up.

Justin stood and walked over to him. "You aren't one to call my sister a whore. You cheated on her, knocked up your yoga instructor and then left when she went out for groceries."

"I came here today to get my family back. Now, I know the real reason you won't take me back." He crossed his arms, glaring at Honor.

"There are a thousand reasons why I don't want to take you back. None of which are another man. Though no one would fault me if I found someone better." Honor spat back.

Steve stared at Honor with a smirk. He reached behind him and opened the door. Henry and Willa stood with tears in their eyes. He grabbed her hand and they ran from the room.

"Henry! Willa!" Honor yelled and ran after the two. Pushing Steve to the side as she passed.

"You really are an asshole. How could you do that to your kids?" I asked.

"Who are you? Just another clinger for the Remington money?" he snarled.

"Excuse me?" I blanched at his accusation.

"Vivienne was right about you. Just another dumb whore that Justin is playing with."

My retort didn't even leave my mouth when Justin's fist collided with Steve's jaw. "That was for my sister."

After the punch, he kneed him in the balls making him double over. Steve writhed on the floor. "That was for my niece and nephew who deserve better than a scumbag like you for a father."

With a kick to the stomach, Justin said, "That's for Cierra. She's a better person than all of us." Justin kneeled down to his ear and whispered, "If I were you, I'd never show your face here again."

I was frozen. Seeing Justin beat Steve up was both frightening and exciting. Justin turned to me and held out his hand. My eyes caught on his battered knuckles as he beckoned me to go with him. Without hesitation, I linked my fingers with his.

He kissed my fingers, and we stepped over the still-prone Steve.

CHAPTER 34

$\mathcal{V}$ivienne stormed into the kitchen. Her gasp echoed off the walls. "What did you do?" she screamed.

"I did what I've been dying to do for years." Justin said.

Rage masked her face. "How dare you? This was your influence, wasn't it?"

I blinked. "I don't know what you are talking ab—"

The slap stung my cheek. It took me a moment to realize she'd backhanded me. I was so stunned I didn't know what to do. Tears burned my eyes from the pain throbbing in my cheek.

She raised her hand again to slap me. Involuntarily, I flinched waiting for the slap. The sound of skin on skin was all that came.

I pried my eyes open. Justin was holding his mother's wrist.

"Don't you ever hit her again." Justin growled in his mother's face.

"You would hit your own mother?" she cried.

"No, but I won't let you hit the woman I love either." He threw her arm down. We walked out of the kitchen.

"Are you ready now?" he asked angrily.

"Yes." I said quietly.

We gathered our jackets and walked toward the door.

"If you leave with her, I don't ever want to see you here again." his mother screeched.

Honor was half-way down the stairs watching her mother. "What is going on?"

"I'm sorry, Honor. We need to go. Give the kids Christmas kisses from me." Justin said.

"Ok." Honor said sadly.

Justin shielded me from his family, an avenging angel made real. I placed my hand on his shoulder and stepped around him.

Honor finished her decent down the stairs. We met in the middle and hugged.

"I have gifts for the kids." I whispered in her ear.

"It's ok. They have plenty." A protest rose on my lips. She gave me a sad smile then said, "But, if you insist we can hang out soon."

Tears blurred my vision. Justin hugged his sister. He whispered something that caused her to nod. A wicked smile crossed her face before Justin walked back to me.

"Merry Christmas, Mother." Justin said with his back to her.

He grabbed my hand and we walked out the door.

THE DRIVE NORTH was filled with silence. Justin's face would go from relaxed to pinched with anger and back again. His fingers flexed on the wheel. At times I thought he was going to dent it. Only a few times I felt the need to talk, but the anger and sadness flowing off of him had me holding my tongue.

Snow-covered trees passed by in a blur. A blanket of peace and calm settled outside. Animals seemed to know it was Christmas Eve. They kept out of sight as the car sped by.

"I'm sorry." His gravelly voice broke the silence.

Turning in my seat, I stared at him.

He sighed. "I'm sorry I put you through that. I've probably ruined everything including Christmas." The steering wheel took an angry hit.

When he went to hit it again, I grabbed his hand and linked our fingers. I bent my head and kissed his sore knuckles.

"I'm impressed." I smiled at him.

"What?" He glanced at me while trying to keep his eyes on the road.

"Two and a half hours of brooding. I usually only get that when I watch a movie."

A smile cracked his angry shell.

"I heard women find broody sexy."

"I don't know who told you that, but it's ok." I teased.

Honestly, I was starting to get worried. Not that I'd tell him that.

"Are we there yet?" He whined with a smirk popping his dimple at me.

"I thought you knew where you were going. You've been doing fine."

He brought my hand to his mouth for a kiss.

"Alright. Yes, we are almost there. Only a few more miles. My parents weren't expecting us this early. I hope they're home." I looked at my phone. "They haven't responded to any of my texts."

"If they aren't home, you can show me around your home town." He suggested.

As we turned down the road that led to my childhood home, I couldn't help but compare the homes I'd seen earlier in the day. All of these houses had outdoor lights of all variety, any inflatable you can imagine, and moving decorations everywhere.

"Wow" Justin slowed the car looking at all the lights.

"They go overboard around here."

"This is great. I wish this had been my neighborhood growing up." A note of sadness echoed through his words.

Justin pulled into my parent's driveway. White lights outlined the small cape cod. An inflatable penguin moved in the breeze. The decorations were pretty tame compared to the rest of the street.

Jumping out of the car, excitement filled me with anticipation of Christmas with my family. Conscientious of my fall earlier, I gingerly walked up the walkway to the front door. Justin followed close behind carrying our bags.

From the porch, I saw lights were on inside the house. I knocked on the door and waited. When there wasn't an answer after the first round of knocks I knocked again. *What could they be doing?* I looked over at Justin and shrugged. Before walking away, I tried the knob. The cold brass turned easily in my hand.

Walking through the door, I listened to see if I could locate Mom and Dad. I left Justin standing by the door while I looked for them. My first look into the living room made me regret all my choices. I immediately turned around and ran outside.

"What's wrong?" Justin followed.

"I need bleach now." I screeched. In my haste to exit my parent's house I didn't pay attention to the walkway. My feet went out from under me when I ran in front of the car.

"Are you ok?" He dropped the bags and kneeled next to me.

"I will never be ok again." I covered my face with my arm.

"Cierra?" Mom's voice called from the door.

"She slipped and fell again." Justin explained.

"Again?" Dad's voice rang out.

"She fell at my mother's house earlier."

"Well, that sounds like Cierra." He dad chimed.

"Are they dressed?" I asked Justin.

He paused. "Uh yes. Why wouldn't they be?"

"Cause they were going at it like two bunnies when I walked in."

Silence filled the air.

"Justin?" I lifted my arm from my eyes.

His lips were pressed together holding back a laugh.

"It's not funny!"

A loud boisterous laugh broke from him.

I smacked him. Rolling up to my knees, I stood on my wobbly legs.

Mom and Dad were standing together at the door. Mom wore a robe with flowers on it. Dad had on gray sweatpants.

"Are you ok, sweetie?" Mom asked.

"No. I will never be the same." I said dramatically.

"Did you hit your head? Do you need to go to the hospital? Jerry get your keys we will take her." Mom walked into the house.

"I don't need to go to the hospital, Mom."

"Then what is wrong?" Mom threw her hands in the air.

"Ugh! I saw you and Dad going at it."

"What?" she shrieked.

"Yep. I will never be the same."

"Oh please. It's not like you're a virgin, Cierra. I'm sure you and your boytoy have gone at it already," Dad said.

"Oh dear Lord." I felt my face flame.

"I'm sure you've said that to him." Dad winked at Justin and walked into the house.

We stood slack-jawed as my parents disappeared into the house.

CHAPTER 35

*M*y body was screaming to get off my feet.

Justin carried our bags up to my childhood bedroom. We stood awkwardly in the bright pink room. Posters of teen heartthrobs, bands, and young actors hung on the walls. A corkboard had photos of friends and boyfriends making up a collage of my high school years.

"Wow! This is like stepping into a time capsule." Justin stared at a few of the trophies on a shelf.

"Yeah. Being an only child my parents, or rather my mom feels the need to keep my room just like it was when I left for college."

Justin's eyes bulged. "I don't think my mother has a sentimental bone in her body."

"I got that from her."

"So, what does your dad want to do with this room?"

"That's a great question, Justin. I'd love to turn this into my own man cave. I could see putting a giant TV over there. I have my eye on a new recliner. We definitely have to paint over this horrible pink." Dad walked around my room.

"Jerry! You are not getting rid of Cierra's room. We never know when she may have to move home."

"Good Lord! You aren't moving home are you?" Dad had a horrified look on his face.

"No. Especially if you and mom are going at it all over the house."

A devious smile crossed his face.

"Jerry." Mom warned.

Dad strode out of the room before he went down the hall to their room he said, "Good thing you don't have a black light."

"Eww."

"Jerry!"

Justin laughed as my parents went to their bedroom. After shutting my door, I began unpacking my bag. Bedsprings squeaked when Justin sat. I looked over to where he sat. He patted the bed.

"Come sit down."

I sucked in a huge gulp of air. My heart flipped in my chest. Walking over to the bed, I sat next to him. His arms snaked around me pulling me close.

"Oh God!" He mumbled into my hair.

"Yeah. Not exactly the best Christmas Eve."

"No, but we do need to talk. I don't want to go another second without getting what is between us out in the open."

My head fell to his chest. A groan escaped me. He tilted my head so my eyes met his.

"I love you. I can't say I understand why you freaked out the other night when I said that, but I want you to know I didn't say it for you to say it back. You are the best thing that has ever come into my life."

"Dammit."

Justin shrunk back as if I'd just hit him.

I sighed. "You are such a wonderful man, Justin. You have done things for me that no man has ever done for me. I freaked out when you said that because I was worried you said it in the spur of the moment. I couldn't handle if that were the case because I had just figured out myself that I am completely in love with you."

His eyes glistened in the moonlight streaming in from my window. Slowly, he moved toward me. Taking my face in his hands, our lips pressed together. It was sweet with a promise of more.

I pushed against his chest. We needed to stop before we couldn't.

"I don't want to do this in my parents' house," I grimaced. An arrant thought of my parents using my room as their playground made me shudder.

"I'm ok with that. I'm warning you though. I will be holding you all night. My Christmas will start with the one person I need in my life." Justin brushed his lips against my temple.

I bit my bottom lip holding back the emotions that were flooding me. But, I felt a wetness drip onto my cheek. Justin reached up and caught the tear.

Crying wasn't something I did.

"Get changed. We want to make sure we are asleep before Santa comes," he winked.

Each of us changed quickly into pajamas. Crawling into bed we laid facing each other. I reached over and ran my hand over his face. His eyes close with my light touch.

"I'm scared." My soft voice carried in the darkness.

Those beautiful eyes stared at me.

"About the last time we were together? I'm so sorry about that."

The huge weight lifted off my chest. I'd been carrying a rock of worry for days.

"I'm not always consistent in taking my pill." I confessed.

"Ok. If something unexpected happens, we will deal with it." Strong hands caressed my back soothing my worries away.

"Ok."

He bit his lip. I could tell he was fighting with himself about revealing something. Flipping on my side, he snuggled against me. A hard bulge rubbed against my butt.

"No bump and grind." I said with a yawn.

"I know, baby. He can't help himself. When you're around, he's happy." My hips were pulled against his to prove his point.

"Good night, Justin."

"Good night, my love."

The heaviness of sleep weighed down on me. However, there was one more thing I needed to say to him. "My Christmas wish came true when I met you."

A lightly pressed kiss to my hair was the last thing I felt before the welcoming void of sleep.

CHAPTER 36

*T*he smell of bacon wafted into my room. A grumbling from my stomach finally woke me up. I stretched my arms over my head. The spot where Justin should be was cold. Reluctantly, I got out of bed. Voices floated upstairs. I padded down the stairs skipping all the spots I knew squeaked.

Mom sat at the kitchen table drinking a cup of coffee. She stared into the kitchen where the voices were. Her eyes met mine and she put one finger to her mouth. On tiptoes, I went over and stood next to her.

Dad and Justin were busy in the kitchen. It was tradition that my dad made Christmas breakfast. It was the one meal he made every year. But, this year it appeared he had an assistant.

"Isn't this cute?" Mom whispered behind her coffee cup.

Justin was busy cutting onions for the fried potatoes while Dad cooked bacon.

"How did this happen?" When Mom didn't answer right away, I looked at her. She was blushing.

"Oh God! What happened now?"

She waved her hand. "Oh nothing. Justin may have caught us in the kitchen."

I felt the color drain from my face. "What?"

"Oh, it was nothing. We were pretty much dressed."

There went my appetite.

"Dear Lord. Can't you two behave for one day?"

"I'm sure we weren't the only ones have a little Christmas nookie," she winked.

"Uh. Yeah you were. We didn't want to do that in my childhood bedroom."

She looked into her coffee mug. "Huh. That never stopped your father and I."

That's it I need new parents.

Not needing any more information about my parents, I went back upstairs to shower and dress.

As I brushed my hair out after my shower a face appeared in my mirror. Justin placed his chin on my shoulder. Wrapping his arms around my towel-covered body he kissed my neck.

I bit my lip holding back a moan.

"Breakfast is ready." His hand wandered down my body.

"Ok. I will be down in a moment."

He met my eyes in the mirror. Leaning down he took my lobe into his mouth. His soft bite sent shivers down my body.

"I locked the door. I'd like to have my breakfast up here," he said, kissing down my neck. I angled my neck to give him better access.

His hands loosened the towel. It fell to the carpet.

"We need to be quick and quiet." I said turning in his arms.

"I can do the quick, but you have to do the quiet." Lifting me up, he carried me over to my bed.

I lay back spread before him. He knelt between my legs. His hands ran up the outside of my legs. Leaning up on my elbows, I watched his caresses. Those blue depths watched me watching him. The desire was like a blue flame.

His mouth lowered to my core blowing on my sensitive flesh sent a shiver through me. His eyes never left mine for his first taste. One long slow lick. A thrill shot through me. I threw my head back and moaned.

"Shh. You have to be quiet or I can't keep doing this." He flicked my swollen clit.

I frantically grabbed a pillow to stifle the moans. With that, he no longer took things slow. Using his fingers in my pussy and his tongue teasing my clit, he pushed me so close to the edge.

My orgasm was so close, but I couldn't get there. The pillow managed to muffle my pleas. Justin must have known what I was asking for because he was relentless trying to get me there. I was about to give up when he dipped his index finger into my wetness.

"Wha—" The words evaded me when he pushed that finger into my puckered virgin hole.

Stars shot through my vision. An orgasm the likes I'd never had before had me shaking and screaming into the pillow. The next thing I knew Justin was lifting the pillow off my face with a smug smile.

"Good for you?" he asked.

"I think you were trying to kill me."

"No, sweetness. I just love watching you come. Now, get dressed we have already been up here too long."

I shot up and ran to my duffle bag. Throwing clothes on, I looked at Justin.

"How do you seem unaffected by all this?"

"Oh babe, I am very much affected but having walked in on your parents doing the horizontal mambo helps." He grimaced.

A groan escaped while I pulled my hair into a low ponytail.

We marched down the steps making enough noise just in case my parents decided to have a little action while waiting for us.

A deep laugh came from the dining room. "It's all clear. No need to walk like you're a herd of elephants." Dad was finishing his plate of food.

"What took you so long, dear?" Mom asked.

"I took a long shower. Sorry."

"Well, sit down and eat so we can exchange presents." Mom waved to the dishes on the table.

Each of us grabbed a plate and piled them high with eggs, potatoes, bacon, sausage and toast. My stomach growled so loudly all eyes turned to me. Ignoring the looks, I shoveled food into my mouth and moaned.

This I missed.

We talked to my parents about the night before. The Christmas Eve dinner that turned out wonderfully with Henry and Willa. Justin's mother's hatred of me even being close to her son. My voice quivered, and Justin squeezed my leg in silent support.

Mom asked how the job was going. It felt a little awkward to be completely honest when my boss was sitting next to me. Justin shrugged as if it was okay for me to be candid. We gave them both details about the upcoming ball. Justin invited them to the final. I was shocked because I hadn't even thought about inviting them.

After breakfast, Mom insisted we finally exchange gifts. She wouldn't let Justin and I wash the dishes beforehand. We all gathered in the living room near the tree. My parents sat on the loveseat near the tree. I sat cross-legged in front of it. It was the same way I'd spent every Christmas morning of my life. Justin joined me by plopping down.

"Justin! Catch!" Dad threw him a red ball.

Justin shook it open to show a Santa hat. "What is this for?"

"You get to play Santa today. Start handing out presents." Dad clapped his hands.

Dutifully, Justin put on the hat and crawled under the tree. He was methodical. Handing each present to the correct recipient.

Afterwards, we dove right in to opening them. Dad opened his presents with the fanfare of someone being led to the gallows. The underwear and socks he got every year were nothing new to him. When he opened an envelope Justin had given him, he got pale.

"What is it, Dad?"

"Season tickets to the Dragos."

"Hockey?"

Dad looked at them closer. "Wait a minute. Two season passes?"

"Yep. I saw how much you loved them. I thought you'd want to take someone, too." Justin smiled.

"Thank you," he said softly.

Unbeknownst to Justin, I had bought my Dad a Dragos jersey. Now, he had the tickets to match.

Mom opened her gifts a lot slower. She enjoyed seeing the faces of everyone opening the presents. Her gifts consisted of scarves and gloves that she loved. However, when she got to her own envelope she dropped it like it burnt her.

"What now?"

"Ireland?"

Justin smiled. "I remember hearing you talk about that when you were visiting Cierra."

"Oh sweetheart!" Mom came over and gave Justin a massive hug. She leaned toward me. "Keep this one." She said to me.

I blushed.

Justin had a few presents himself. When Mom found out Justin was going to be coming with me, she knew she wanted to get him a few small things. Justin received cufflinks, a gorgeous tie and a bottle of wine. I didn't bring my gift with me because I wasn't quite sure where we were on the gift giving.

While opening my presents, I leaned over to him. "I have something for you but I left it at home."

"I don't need anything as long as I have you," he whispered. "The only present I wanted I already got to unwrap today."

I blushed again.

Ugh! I hated how this man could do that to me.

"Open yours."

The expression on his face I couldn't read. He looked nervous.

I took the envelope in my hand. Slowly ripping it open everyone watched my reaction. When I pulled out the paper, my jaw dropped.

"What is it?" Mom squirmed in her seat like an excited puppy.

"It's a plane ticket."

"For what?"

"It says Sicily."

"Well, it's actually for a flight to get onto a cruise around the Mediterranean."

Just when I thought I could compose myself, my jaw dropped again.

"Justin, this is too much."

"I want to make your dreams come true. sweetheart. I have the means, let me spoil you a little." He kissed me to punctuate his comment. "I bought more than one ticket. You can take whoever you'd like Trina, Dinah or . . ."

"You?"

"I was hoping, but I wanted you to have the choice. You aren't obligated to take me."

"Cierra, you better take that boy." Mom said.

A huge smile crossed my face. "I believe I will."

CHAPTER 37

he rest of Christmas was filled with embarrassing stories about my childhood. Justin, being a gentleman, listened to my parents' cringing anecdotes and sexual innuendos. When Mom threatened to bring out the photo albums I took it as our cue to leave.

We bid my parents farewell. They promised to be at the ball. Justin promised to come back to see Mom in *Rent*. Buying earplugs were still on my to-do list before that day came.

The drive back to the city was comfortably quiet. It was difficult to understand the level of comfort we had. Our connection was as if we'd known each other for years, but the reality was we've only known one another for a month.

"What is going on in that head of yours." Justin asked as we entered the city.

"Nothing. I was just thinking about how much I have to do when we get back."

"The ball?"

"Yes and no. The caterer and media are up in the air. Not to mention the conference at the beginning of January."

Justin nodded. His hand slid to my knee and squeezed.

I turned in my seat to watch him drive. His handsome face was alight with the sun streaming in. The beauty he possessed took my breath away. He pulled into a parking spot outside of my apartment.

He quickly got out of his car and opened my door. We grabbed our bags and gifts making our way into the building.

It was quiet. With the snow and the holiday atmosphere it felt lite.

Digging through my bag, I found my keys. The door swung open with a cool breeze hitting me.

"Oh boy! I must have turned the heat down lower than I thought." I went over to the thermostat to adjust the heat.

Justin shut the door behind him. He quietly came up behind me. Strong arms encircled me.

"I love being like this with you." I spun in his arms, locking my arms around his neck.

"Like what?"

"Just being us. No one else around. No responsibilities. No crazy family. Being Cierra and Justin feels so good. I think I may be addicted."

A chill shot over me. I wasn't sure if it was the low heat or the words he said.

I gave him a devilish look. "Let's finish what we started earlier."

My lips met his in an urgent kiss. He picked me up with his hands under my butt. Wrapping my legs around his waist, I could feel his hardness already.

"Merry Christmas to me." He kissed me hard carrying me to my bedroom.

"THIS HAS DEFINITELY BEEN A MEMORABLE CHRISTMAS." Justin said running his hands through my sex mussed hair.

"I agree. At least the sex has been good." I listened to his heart thudding under my ear.

"Just good?"

I couldn't help rolling my eyes. Typical man. "Eh . . . it was alright."

"Oh so now it's just alright."

Justin tickled my sides. I squirmed and squealed. Getting away wasn't an option when he rolled on top of me and pinned my hands over my head.

"Do you want to change your answer, Ms. Jameson?" His hips rolled against my core. He was ready for another round.

"Hmm. I may need some convincing." My tongue traced up his neck causing him to shiver.

"I think I can be very convincing." A giggle escaped. His eyes turned bright with desire.

Three hours later and two more rounds of incredible sex, I was brushing my hair. One of our rounds found us in the shower, which ended on the bathroom floor. A delicious ache had me biting back a moan with each movement.

Justin was lounging on my bed watching me braid my damp hair. A satisfied smirk played on his lips. His arrogance when it came to sex was astounding. However, he could follow through so I didn't fault him.

"Don't you look like the cat that ate the canary?"

When the braid was finished, I walked over to the bed. His hands shot out and pulled me back on the bed.

"Don't tell me you want another round?" I cuddled into his embrace.

"With you, I'm insatiable." A noticeable bulge was showing through his jeans.

His warmth had my eyes drooping. Sleep was pulling me under. I fought it. Every moment with Justin felt unique. I didn't want to miss anything.

"Sleep, baby. I'll be here when you wake."

"Okay."

When I awoke a bit later, I was still wrapped around Justin. He was reading a book. Blinking the sleep out of my eyes, I read the title. My face flamed. It was one of the romance novels I had on my bedside table. A favorite of mine. The worn cover and dog-eared pages were proof.

"This is interesting reading." He said looking down at me.

"You like romance?" A crooked grin made me think of all the naughty things we've done.

"Truthfully, I've never read one of these books. But, this has given me a lot of insight into you. Apparently, you like longhaired pirates who quote, "'ravage the damsel with his long hard member.'"

"Oh God!"

"Don't be embarrassed, babe. I'm actually getting some fantastic ideas."

I smacked his hard abs. "Stop teasing."

"We could go to a costume shop and pick up a pirate costume for me and a wench costume for you. I'd love to board you."

I groaned at his corny joke.

When he wiggled his eyebrows trying to be sexy, I burst into a fit of giggles.

"Alright, Captain. Are you hungry? We could order Chinese."

"Sounds good." He placed the book back on the nightstand.

As he stood, I remembered his gift.

"Wait!" Springing up, I ran out to retrieve the small gift I bought for him.

"What is this?" He looked at the small box.

"Open it and see."

He ripped into the wrapping paper. A look of awe crossed his face.

"I wasn't sure if we were at the gift giving part of our relationship. So, it isn't terribly extravagant."

"I love it." He held up the keychain with the band Halestorm's logo. Then he saw there was something else in there. Tickets to their next concert were folded at the bottom of the box.

"Are you kidding me right now? I didn't even know they were touring. This is fantastic."

"You like it? I'm sure you could get better seats." He shook his head.

"If you're with me at this concert, then it doesn't matter where the hell we sit." He pulled me to him planting an epic kiss on my lips.

My stomach took that moment to grumble. "Let's get food before you start to become hangry."

I swatted him, but he jumped out of my reach. He ran to the kitchen to find the take out menu.

CHAPTER 38

"*J*anice, please bring me the list of attendees for the Ride a
Horse gala."

"Yes, Ms. Jameson." Janice's clipped voice rang
through my intercom.

My attention was on the screen in front of me. We were two days
away from the ball and everything was finally coming together. A
figure walked into my office. Assuming it was Janice, I didn't look up
from my program.

"Thank you, Ja—" A lump formed in my throat when I saw who
was in my office.

"Janice went on break." Vivienne Remington sat across from my
desk.

"Hello, Mrs. Remington. What can I do for you today?"

Her steely gaze bored into me. She sat ramrod straight and rang her
hands in her lap. An impeccable suit of gray made her the epitome of
elegance.

"Ms. Jameson, I have come for a very specific reason."

My heart threatened to pound out of my chest. Vivienne Remington
never did anything without a purpose. Every possible reason for her
appearance ran through my head.

"I have come to apologize."

That wasn't one of them.

"Excuse me." I sat back in my chair.

She looked down at her hands. "Have you ever loved someone so much that if you lost them, part of you would die?"

Until I'd met Justin, I would have said no. The more I am with him, the more I can't see a life without him.

"Not until recently." I said.

"That is how I felt about Justin's father. We had a lot of ups and downs. Money was never an issue, however, with money comes complications. My world crumbled when he died." A lone tear rolled down her cheek.

I handed her the box of tissue I kept in my desk drawer.

"What does this have to do with me?"

"Selfishly, I didn't want my family to feel the pain of losing someone like that. That is why I pushed Sicora on Justin. I know they aren't suited. In fact, she is a spoiled brat. But if he never felt the amount of love I had then, he'd never feel the pain either."

Anger burned through me. "That is ridiculous. You can't control people's lives like that. You would rather him live an unhappy life with someone he wouldn't care deeply for, than a happy one even if in the end there was pain?"

Vivienne Remington stared at me.

"Why are you *really* here, Vivienne?"

She took several deep breaths. It seemed she was giving herself an internal pep talk. "I need your help."

I waited.

"I made a big mistake on Christmas Eve. My children aren't talking to me. Justin won't take my calls. Honor won't let me see Henry or Willa."

"Why does all this matter all of a sudden? You were pretty steadfast in your opinions on Christmas Eve."

"After you and Justin left, Honor packed up the kids. Steve and Sicora hit it off and disappeared not long after. I was alone. My once bustling home full of Christmas cheer and excitement was now a tomb. A tomb I created for myself. I know I did all of this. I let my grief ruin my family. They are all I have now, Cierra. Please help me get them back." She begged.

"What do you want me to do?"

She deflated. "I don't know. I'm sorry I even came."

She stood and walked toward the door.

"Vivienne, I will see if I can come up with anything." I said.

Without turning toward me, she said, "Thank you."

"Don't thank me yet. If I am able to arrange something, it will be up to you to fix things."

Vivienne nodded and walked out of my office. Janice walked in after she left with a smug smile on her face. She handed me the list of attendees and walked out.

The names in front of me blurred as the tears pricked my eyes. Vivienne Remington wouldn't shed a tear for me. When I thought about Honor, Justin, Henry, and Willa, my heart broke. Their relationships were so different from what I knew. I wanted to help them.

Looking down at the papers in front of me, an idea emerged. A smile curved my lips as I set about helping the Remington family.

WE WERE ONLY a day away from the ball. Everything was in place to make it an incredible success for Jonas. Dinah, Honor, Trina, and I were hunting for the best dress to stun everyone into submission. What they didn't know was I'd already found my dress and it was going to have Justin panting after me all night. I smiled at that idea.

Trina had insisted we all have a girls' day out and find our dresses for the gala. Unfortunately, being the planner for said gala I still had a lot of work to do. So, being the queen of multi-tasking I brought my laptop along to our shopping expedition.

"What do you think about this one?" Trina's voice brought my attention back to her.

"It's nice." I looked back down to the laptop in my lap.

"Will you shut that damn thing?" Dinah reached over to shut it, but I yanked it away before she could.

"I just need to finish a few emails then my attention is back to you." I explained.

"Uh huh. She's right though, Trina. That dress is meh at best."

Trina twirled in front of the three-way mirror. The dress she was wearing was worse than meh. The color and cut looked horrible on her.

"Alright. Let me try the next one on." Walking back into her dressing room, she knocked on the door next to hers and said, "come on, Honor."

Honor walked out with a floor-length peach gown. It had sequins across the bodice that was held up with spaghetti straps.

"Wow!" Dinah and I said together.

"Is that a good wow?" She stared at us then back to herself smoothing down the gown around her hips.

We nodded.

"That is the dress for you." She blushed and walked back to the fitting room with a bounce in her step.

"Come on, Trina. Number 5,845 should be our winner." Dinah called.

"If this one doesn't work, I'm just not going." She stepped in front of the mirrors again.

Dinah and I gaped at our best friend.

"Oh my God!" I breathed.

When I looked over at Dinah she had tears in her eyes. Trina was breathtaking. She wore a black dress, but it wasn't your typical LBD. A fitted bodice flowed into an A-line skirt. The bodice had intricate embroidery scattered with sequins that glinted in the overhead lights. This was Trina's perfect dress.

"If you don't buy that dress right now, I may have to kill you." Dinah choked out.

Trina blushed and rushed back into the dressing room.

"You two are up next." Honor sat next to me with her peach gown draped over her arm.

"I don't have to. I already found my dress." I said while concentrating on the screen in my lap.

Honor and Dinah's heads snapped to me.

Trina swung open the dressing room door half naked. "What?" she asked.

"I found my perfect gown already." I shrugged.

"So, we wasted our time today?"

"Absolutely not. Dinah still needs to find her perfect dress." I looked over at Trina. "You need to finish getting dressed."

Her face flamed when she realized she was standing there in a strapless bra and spanx.

"Why do I need a dress? I am working with the catering." Dinah huffed.

"You aren't just helping by supplying pastries. You are an invited guest. Now, get your ass up and try on those dresses." I snapped my fingers at her.

An hour later, Trina, Honor and Dinah paid for their dresses. They planned on leaving their dresses with me to leave at the hotel. I had reserved us a room with the promise of some pre-game cocktails while we dressed to impress.

As part of my job, I was responsible for the setup of the event. I found myself over at the hotel talking with the vendors and hotel staff. All had guaranteed everything was going according to plan. Doing a final check of the room, I was filled with pride. It was all coming together. If I could pull this off, I would be illustrating just how valuable I was as WTR's corporate event planner.

As I left the hotel, my phone vibrated in my purse. A text flashes on my screen.

Mr. McSexyPants: Hello beautiful

My body flushed every time he said that.

Me: Just left the hotel

Mr. McSexyPants: Everything coming together?

Me: Yep.

Dots appeared next to Justin's nickname. The dots blinked while I waited for his reply. He was taking too long to respond so, I put my phone away to focus on walking back to my apartment. It had begun to snow. When I shivered, I pulled my wool jacket tighter around me. The vibrations coming from my purse, forced me to step under an awning outside of a deli to check the message.

Mr. McSexyPants: Did you and girls find your dresses today?

I furrowed my brow. This text conversation was starting to feel forced.

Me: Yep.

Me: What is going on?

The dots appeared again. I huffed in frustration. It was loud enough to draw the attention of a couple walking by.

Mr. McSexyPants: I miss you?

Me: Are you asking me?

I laughed.

Mr. McSexyPants: No. I miss you.

Mr. McSexyPants: Where are you right now?

Me: Under an awning and I'd like to start moving before I freeze to death

"Hello Beautiful" A deep voice whispered in my ear. I spun and punched the guy in the throat.

My purse was held up like a shield. A few ragged breaths, calmed me instantly. The guy I'd just throat punched was hunched over wheezing. It was Justin.

"Holy shit! Are you ok?" I rubbed his back.

"Didn't. Know. You'd. Kill. Me." Each word was punctuated with a gasping of air.

"I'm so sorry. I go into fight mode when someone sneaks up on me in the street."

Justin slowly stood. His face was an unflattering purple color. I bit my lip trying not to laugh as he recovered from the hit.

"Good" he said a bit more clearly.

"What the hell are you doing here?" I asked.

"Well, I went to pick you up at the hotel to take you home but you'd left already. I didn't want you walking home in this snow."

His car sat idling a half a block up from where we were standing.

"I'm so sorry. Are you ok now?"

He nodded. His warm hand sat on my lower back and guided me over to his idling car.

As he opens the door, I feel the warmth from inside hit my face. If my body could have moaned, it would have been embarrassingly loud and long. I hadn't realized how cold I was until I sat in his warm car.

However, it was the glorious seat warmers that actually had me moaning.

A smug smile crossed his face.

"That good huh?"

"Yes. I may marry your seat warmers. They are heaven."

"Never thought I'd see the day I was jealous of an inanimate object."

"No need to be jealous. I'd love if we got a move on it though. It's getting late, and we both have a big day tomorrow."

"Your wish is my command, m'lady." He smirked and sped his car into traffic.

CHAPTER 39

"Where is the damn curling iron?" Dinah yelled from the bathroom.

She, Honor and Trina had shown up a few minutes ago. Chao reigned with all of the hair products, make-up, shoes, dresses and anything else women may need to prepare for a big party. I watched as they all scuttled around. Trina had curlers in her hair, Honor had just a slip on with her hair partially pinned up, and Dinah was trying to put make-up on while Trina and Honor attempted to do something with her gray and blue hair.

"Are you going to start getting ready?" Trina asked.

"I will. I am just enjoying my cocktail before I do." Three pairs of eyes swiveled to the drink in my hand.

"There is fucking alcohol here?" Trina stormed away from the mirror.

"Yes." I pointed to the selection I had on a table.

"We have been here for more than 15 minutes and you are just now telling us." Honor made herself a rum and coke.

"The three of you came in here like Tasmanian devils. I didn't have a chance."

There was a knock at the door. Dinah opened it without seeing who was there. My mom and dad waltzed in like they owned the place. Dad spied the liquor and made a beeline.

Mom clapped her hands. "Alright girls, let's get started."

"Mom, why are you up here?"

"Justin told me which room all of you were getting ready in. I just knew you all would need my help. So, here we are."

I looked over at my dad. He sat next to me. "I'm here for this." He lifted his drink in salute.

Downing my drink, I entered the melee.

I TOOK one last look before I grabbed my clutch and room key. Everyone else had left and headed down to the ball. My hair was perfectly curled and bouncy. Eyes were smoky with just the right amount of sexy. The royal blue satin dress hung on me like a dream. Off the shoulder with a plain bodice brought elegance and professionalism. I was still working after all.

Closing the door behind me, I walked to the elevator. My stilettos made muted clicks on the carpet. The doors opened with an empty car. I watched the floors tick by as butterflies somersaulted. This ball was important in so many ways. I needed to save Jonas's shelter. I needed to show all my doubters that I could do this job.

Well, none of that calmed me down. All I needed now was a brown paper bag to help me breathe.

The elevator doors opened to the busy lobby. It was go time.

Shoulders back.

Head up.

Boobs out.

Walk slowly so the damned shoes wouldn't have you falling in front of everyone.

Taking a deep breath, I entered the bustling lobby. Beautifully dressed people were everywhere.

Why weren't they in the ballroom?

Panic raced through me. I walked quickly through the throng of people. Nodding a hello to those who called out my name. I met the hotel's planner outside the door.

"What is going on?" I whispered.

"I'm sorry. We had a last-minute adjustment. The doors will be open shortly."

I looked around at all the wealthy and annoyed attendees. "Get servers out here with champagne now."

She nodded then scurried out.

"Everything ok?" Jonas asked.

"Yes. Apparently they weren't quite ready for us." A flat smile crossed my face.

"Dear God, that is a frightening smile. If you keep looking like that, I'm not going to raise the money we need," Jonas joked.

"You aren't funny." I gritted out. Servers wove around to the waiting attendees. Smiles reappeared. I relaxed slightly.

"Don't worry. You got this." Jonas kissed my cheek and walked toward some people I didn't recognize.

Doors finally opened. The sharp-dressed crowd flowed into the room. Gasps could be heard from my place by the door. People continued in while I greeted those I knew.

Within the throng, Jonas walked with Dinah. A sweet blush colored her cheeks. He took her hand and looped it in his arm. I caught his eye, and he winked.

"Never thought I'd see that." Dean's voice said from next to me.

I jumped. Smiling I hugged Dean and Sean. "I didn't know you guys were coming. I'm so happy you are here."

"Sweetie, we would never miss this. This is the reason we haven't been seeing you." Sean looked over my shoulder. "Well, one of the reasons."

I turned to see what he was looking at. The most gorgeous man I'd ever seen was walking toward me. His tuxedo was custom-fitted.

My mouth had been hanging open while watching him stride over. I clicked my mouth shut. A blush crept up my neck.

His sexier-than-sin smile had me wondering if I should have worn panties.

Then again, he would have burned them off with that look.

"I don't think we are needed around here." Dean touched my shoulder walking inside.

"Wow!" I breathed.

"At least you have a word. I can't find any words to describe you." Justin was so close I could feel the warmth off his body. A shiver shot through me.

"I'm glad you are here." I didn't think I could say anything more stupid. Of course, he was going to be there.

That sexy smirk reappeared. "I have something for you."

He held out a small velvet box. My heart thumped hard in my chest. I was really going to need that paper bag soon.

"Open it." Our fingers touched as I took the box.

I slowly opened the lid. Inside sat a pair of diamond earrings. Not a pair of studs. These diamond earrings had an intricate design that included sapphires.

"Oh my God, Justin. These are gorgeous. I can't accept these." I attempted to push the box back into his hand.

That smirk was back. "Yes, you can. Come on, Cierra. It's not like it's an engagement ring or something."

Thrill and panic flashed through me. The idea of marriage with anyone was never something that interested me.

Looking at this man, all I wanted to do was marry him and have his babies.

"I wouldn't mind that either," Justin said.

Dammit! My inner monologue wasn't working again.

Damn my dad and his shots.

To distract from my unfiltered mouth, I put the earrings on.

"Gorgeous. Just what you needed," he reached out and took my hand. "Shall we."

Nodding, I linked my arm with his.

CHAPTER 40

The room had a soft glow. Lights were muted. Soft music played in the background. Tables were arranged around the room in a semi-circle around a dance floor.

People had found their way to their seats. Others wandered around looking at the posters we had custom made for the event. Each poster had one of the available animals on it with their stories.

There were two bar areas on opposite sides of the large room. As a favor to me, Donny and his brother, Derrick, manned the bars. A long table of treats sat near one of the exits. Dinah designed animal-inspired treats along with some pet treats for the animals there.

Justin and I wandered over to where the animals were. With all the commotion, they were all pretty calm. Obie and Alfie wore doggie tuxedos. The terrible trio was in a cage glaring at all of the passersby. A few of the reptiles and bunnies were also present.

Justin linked our fingers. He pulled me over to see Obie and Alfie.

"There are the two of the most handsome men here." I squatted down to scratch Obie.

"You really love these guys, don't you?" Justin asked.

I nodded with a smile. "Don't tell the rest, but they are my favorite."

"They've been adopted already." Jonas's sister Angie said.

"What?" A wave of sadness overcame me.

"Obie and Alfie were the first ones."

"Oh." I said.

"It was a very generous donation." Angie smiled down at the two dogs.

"Well, that's good, right? Who adopted them?"

Angie patted Obie on the head. "They wanted to be left anonymous."

"Oh, I understand."

"Cierra, we need to work the room." Justin tugged on my hand, pulling me away from Angie and the animals.

Justin and I wove through the crowd stopping here and there to talk. A familiar face started walking toward us. The nerves I had earlier were nothing compared to these.

"Hello, Vivienne." I greeted the elegantly dressed woman.

"Cierra, dear." She looked over my shoulder at Justin. His back was to us.

I tapped his shoulder. His bright smile made me tingle. When his eyes caught who was in front of me, his face fell. He excused himself from the men he was talking with.

"Mother, what are you doing here?" He snapped.

"I wanted to see you, Justin." Vivienne said quietly.

I laid my hand on his arm. "I'm going to leave you to talk. I'll be near the bar."

Before Justin could protest I strode away. Snaking through the throngs of party goers. Approaching the bar, I watched the bartender flipping containers of alcohol filling drinks with a flourish. Donny was busy filling drinks when I managed to find a spot in front of him.. After pouring champagne, he walked over to where I was standing.

"What can I get you, Cierra?"

"A white wine please."

"Here you go." His clipped attitude startled me.

"What's up, Donny?"

"Nothing." He was scowling at something across the room.

Trina was standing by the other bar where Derrick was working.

"Seems like they are getting along."

"He doesn't deserve her." Donny mumbled.

"Oh really? We are back to this then? Who is good enough for her?"

He sighed. His gaze met mine. "I wish I hadn't been so stupid for so long."

"So, what is stopping you from telling her?"

"Telling her what?"

"That you see her."

He shrugged. "I think she and Derrick have something."

My eyes flashed over to the other bar. Trina was looking over and ducked her head.

I squeezed his shoulder. "It's never too late, Donny."

White wine in hand, I moved away from the bar. My eyes found Justin and his mother. They were talking intensely. Honor had found her way over to them and stood there watching her mother and brother talk.

My stomach tightened. If this didn't work out with them, I could lose a boyfriend and a friend for a woman who couldn't stand me.

"Cierra!" Jonas swung me up in his arms.

"Jonas, you big lug! Put me down." I smacked him.

"Jonas, don't be a douche." Dinah walked over with a beer in her hand.

"How do you think things are going?" I asked.

"You know, I don't know. I think they are doing well, but even if they aren't then I can say we went out with a bang." Jonas put his arm around Dinah.

I looked at Dinah with a "what the hell is going on" look. She blushed and shrugged his arm off. He smiled and kissed her forehead.

How long had this been going on?

Dinah moved away and stood next to me. Soon, Trina found her way over with Dean and Sean hot on her heels.

"There is the lady of the evening! You did a fantastic job, sweetie. I always knew you were meant for great things." Dean sniffed, and Sean handed him his hanky.

"Thank you guys! If we don't save the shelter, it will all be for naught."

Silence settled over our little group when the seriousness of the situation sunk in.

A tapping of the mic drew our attention toward the dance floor.

"That's your clue to go sit down. I will catch up with you all later." A quick hug from Dinah and Trina calmed me before walking toward the mic.

Justin was standing by the DJ waiting for me. I smiled as I approached, but Justin wouldn't meet my eyes. My heart sunk while a feeling of dread overcame me.

"Ladies and gentleman, thank you all for coming. Tonight, we are here to raise money for the Ride A Horse Save a Husky animal safe house. I have had my own personal experience with the shelter. I've seen first hand the great work Jonas Williams does with animals that have been at kill shelters. Compared to the woman I am about to introduce, I have very little experience, in fact those cute little kittens you saw back there stole my wallet and keys when I volunteered." A laugh rippled through the crowd. "Cierra Jameson has volunteered for years with this shelter. I saw how much this shelter meant to her and knew I had to do what I could to save it. So, without any further ado, Cierra Jameson."

Justin walked over to where I was standing. He wore a smile that didn't quite meet his eyes.

Planting a kiss on my cheek, he whispered in my ear, "We need to talk."

I plastered a smile on my face and took the mic. It was time to save the shelter.

CHAPTER 41

*N*ineties pop rock echoed through the ballroom. Ladies had their heels kicked off while they danced. Groups of wealthy individuals networked at tables while others continued to utilize the bar.

"You did it." Mom sat next to me. My feet were propped up on the chair next to me. Thanks to my tight shoes, my toes ached as I flexed them.

"What are you talking about, Mom?" I watched Honor, Trina and Dinah doing their best running man.

"Well, you did a few things. First, you put together a phenomenal holiday ball that could help save your friend's business. Second, you saved his business. Third, you tried to help a family come back together." She rubbed my shoulder.

"How do you know about the last thing?"

"I met Vivienne Remington. She apologized to me, and we talked. We talked a lot. In fact, she and I are going to do lunch after the New Year."

"You and Vivienne Remington?"

"I figure I should get to know the woman who will be my daughter's mother in law."

"Oh God, Mom! That is not going to happen. In fact, Justin hasn't talked to me since he talked to her. I think it might be over." Pain lanced through me with that thought.

"Oh honey. If he didn't see a future with you why would he have adopted those dogs?"

I spun in my seat. "What the hell are you talking about, Mother?"

My mother's mouth took the shape of an O. The music changed to a slow song.

"Margaret, I think I need to save you from yourself. Let's dance." Dad pulled Mom out of the seat.

What did Justin do?

"Can I have this dance?" The deep voice that never ceases to give me shivers caressed my ear.

"Yes." I slipped my pinchy heels back on. We walked hand in hand to the dance floor.

Couples swayed to an Adele song.

Justin pulled me close. The heat coming off him relaxed me instantly.

"Now, I get to talk to you."

There went my relaxation.

"Ok."

He chewed on his bottom lip for a minute. It took all my willpower not to kiss him right then.

"You invited my mother."

"I did."

"Why?"

I lifted one shoulder and looked down at my stilettos.

"Yes, you do. Why did you invite the woman who treated you like shit from the time she met you?"

I sighed and pulled him close. "She came to my office last week."

"And . . ."

"And she was broken. She was in pain. I think being alone during the holidays because of what she did snapped something."

"Ok."

"Don't get me wrong. I made her prove to me that this was a good thing. I know how hard it is to deal with the death of a family member.

I also know that for you to lose both of your parents it was hurting you."

He smiled.

I pulled back. My gaze collided with his. "Did I do the right thing?"

Justin swayed me to the music. "Thank you. Mother, Honor, and I had a very intense conversation. I agreed to start talking to her again, but if she ever pulled that crap with me, you or Honor, she would lose us forever."

"Ok."

"I wish you would have told me."

"Justin, I couldn't. All I guaranteed for your mother was that you and Honor would be at the same place as her. I didn't want to risk anything in case she didn't show."

"You really are one of the greatest people I've ever met."

"Does that mean you aren't mad at me anymore?"

His laugh rang through the dance floor. A few couples close to us glanced over.

"Baby, I was never mad at you."

"Why did you ignore me when we welcomed everyone?"

"I didn't. I hate public speaking. It took everything I had to not pass out, puke or both. I was focusing really hard."

A soft laugh escaped. "I was freaked out, too."

His strong arms wrapped around me. My head laid on his shoulder as the ending notes of the song carried through room. A fast drumbeat signaled the end the beginning of a faster song. I pried myself away from Justin but kept my hand in his. We walked back to the table and worked finished our drinks.

"Hey," I turned toward him. "Mom said something really strange. She hinted to me that you knew who adopted Obie and Alfie. Is that true?"

A fierce blush crept up his neck. He adjusted the neck of his tuxedo's shirt as if it was choking him. "I do know."

"Who is it? I want to give them pointers for those boys."

He mumbled something into his hand.

"What?" I asked.

In a barely audible voice he said, "I adopted them."

"You what?"

"I adopted them. The reason the ball didn't open on time was due to me. I wanted to make sure those boys got saved no matter what happened tonight."

"Oh. Well, since we managed to raise a good portion of the money, you don't have to adopt them."

He furrowed his brow. "Don't you want me to adopt them?"

"It's not that, but you have a really busy schedule at times. Plus, you have Rascal."

"I think Rascal would love having two brothers." He smiled. "I was also hoping you'd think about moving in with me."

The alcohol has finally kicked in. There was no way I had just heard what he said.

"Move in with you?"

"Yes. Well, actually I was hoping we could find a brand-new place together. Something that would be ours."

"You have got to be joking. We haven't even been dating a month." I was grasping at straws. My heart was screaming at my head to start packing while my head was counting the reasons it was a bad idea to move in with my boss/boyfriend.

"I don't care how long it has been. All I know is that I need to be with you. Not being able to see you every night kills me."

I bit my lip holding back the YES my heart was begging me to say.

"I need to think about this, Justin."

He nodded. The knowing smile on his face said he knew he was going to get his way even if it wasn't as soon as he'd like.

Justin and I sat at the table while the ball continued on. The music pumped up the dancers, the booze made people looser with their wallets, and I couldn't hide the smile that spread across my face. Watching the good time around us gave me a sense of accomplishment even thought my feet throbbed with their own heartbeat at the moment.

"Who is that?" Justin asked.

My gaze followed where he was pointing. Honor was dancing with a man in an impeccable suit.

"Oh my God! It can't be." I stood and walked toward the edge of the dance floor.

Justin stood next to me with a grimace. "Who is it?"

"It looks like Darren."

"Who is Darren?" He snapped.

"Alright, cut the protective big brother act. He is Donny's brother."

"Wait! Is that the guy you were teasing her about on Christmas Eve?"

"The exact same."

"What the hell is he doing here? Is this something else you set up?" His clipped tone had my hair standing on end.

"I don't know how he got here. He wasn't on the list. No, I didn't set this up no matter what you may think."

Honor noticed her audience. She stopped dancing and walked over to us. Her face looked like a storm was brewing.

"What?" she said.

"Who is that?" Justin snapped.

"Darren." The man in question put his hand out. Justin glared at the outstretched hand.

"Honor, I need to speak with you." He pulled his sister off the dance floor.

Darren and I were left staring at one another. "So, I didn't see your name on the list. How did you get an invite?"

"My partner, Cameron Stevens, was supposed to come. He, uh, had something unexpected come up." Darren looked over at Justin and Honor arguing. "I am glad, however, he couldn't come."

I looked at the very handsome Darren. He was no Justin, but I could see what Honor saw. Worry crossed his features while he watched the siblings.

"You think I need to intervene?" He asked.

Honor walked away from Justin with her hands flung in the air. She was headed toward the bar.

"I don't think that's necessary." He watched her snatch up a glass of champagne. She downed it in one swig. "I'd go get her if I were you."

Darren sped over to her. Justin had an angry look on his face.

"What is your problem?" I asked.

"She doesn't need to be getting involved with someone so soon. Steven would use that against her."

"She is an adult, Justin. She's a mother for chrissakes. Let her be. I don't think she is going to jump into anything."

A sheepish look crossed his features. "I guess you're right."

"Dumbass"

He snapped his head toward me. I raised an eyebrow daring him to question my logic. Justin pulled me into his arms and nuzzled my neck. Relief coursed through my body.

"What do you make of that?" He asked.

"It feels like you want to take me upstairs." I referred to the bulge digging into my hip.

He pulled me tighter and laughed. "That is definitely something I want to do, but I am talking about that."

My eyes scanned the room in front of us. Nothing stood out until I saw two figures in an alcove. "Trina and Donny?" I breathed.

Yep. The two of them were mauling each other. It looked like those two needed to use my room.

"Well, that is an interesting development." Justin kissed down my neck. Nipping lightly as he went. Chills shot through my body heating my core.

"You better stop that."

"I don't think so." With his hand on my back he led me through the thinning crowd. "You have your room key, right?"

I held up my purse, removed my heels and ran toward the elevator like a kid on prom night. His thundering steps followed me into the elevator. No one dared to follow us into the elevator. He pinned me against the wall and kissed me. The kiss felt like he needed it to survive. Breathing didn't matter as long as we had each other.

I knew right then no matter what I wanted this man for as long as I could keep him.

CHAPTER 42

NEW YEAR'S EVE

"There better be a lot of fucking booze tonight." Dinah yelled from my doorway.

"Hi there! Welcome! Please have a drink." With an eye roll, I pointed her toward the drinks.

Dinah glared at me. "You know I hate this stupid celebration. It's just an excuse for people to get drunk. Kiss people you will never see again. Start the new year by waking up on your front stoop with no pants with a cat laying on your head hung-over."

Trina and I stared at Dinah.

"That was oddly specific." Justin said walking from my bedroom with wine in his hands.

I smirked when he ducked away from a swatting Dinah.

"Alright, Dinah, relax it will be fun. Mrs. B is coming over tonight too."

"What?" Dinah shrieked.

"Yes!" Trina cheered.

Dinah and Trina voices mixed together. Dinah looked over at Trina. "You're excited to see that old bitty?"

"I want to be her when I grow up. She is awesome." Trina leaned close to Dinah. "If you're lucky maybe she can give you pointers on being a lonely cat lady."

Dinah humphed and crossed her arms.

"I can definitely give you pointers, dear. Believe me my pussy takes care of me." She winked and carried in a pan of her lasagna. Justin took it from her while she gave me, Trina and Dinah hugs.

"Glad you could make it, Mrs. B."

"Thank you for thinking of an old bitty like me." She smirked at me then stared past me.

I turned and saw Justin was bending over to pick up a piece of trash.

My elderly neighbor was now checking out my boyfriend.

This was going to be one hell of a New Year's Eve party.

"Oh, Justin!" She said waving her hand.

"Yes, Mrs. B."

"Nice work. Keep it up. In more ways then one if you know what I mean." Justin's face turned a shade of red I'd never seen.

Mrs. B. cackled and walked over to where my parents were chatting with Vivienne. Dad saw her walking over. A panicked look crossed his face. He quickly moved to stand by the Christmas tree and pretended to join a conversation with Jonas, Dean and Sean. As she walked by, she pinched my dad's butt. Mom and Vivienne laughed when Dad jumped a foot in the air.

"Is there anything you need us to help with?" Trina asked.

"Justin and I have been busting our asses all day. I'm pretty sure there isn't anything else we need."

"I'm sure you have been "busting your asses all day." Dean walked over to join us. A glass of white wine dangled between his fingers.

"Why do you have to turn everything dirty?" Dinah asked her brother.

A look of mischief floated in his eyes. "Why don't you go talk to Jonas?"

Color drained from Dinah's face. She snapped her head toward where Jonas was still standing with Dad and Sean.

"Did something happen between you and Jonas?" I asked.

She opened and closed her mouth twice. She looked like a fish out of water.

"Did something happen at the ball?" Trina asked.

Dinah glared at us. She snatched Dean's white wine and marched over to sit on the couch.

The three of us giggled. "That was amazing. Something definitely happened." Trina took a sip of her red wine.

Dean and I looked at each other.

"Where is Donny tonight?" I asked.

Trina took a swig of her wine but her eyes darted to me. "How would I know?"

"Well, I thought after the show the two of you put on at the ball he would have been here tonight." I smirked at the blush that rose on her cheeks.

She swallowed twice. "I have no idea what you're talking about."

"Come on, sweetheart. Most of us saw you two. What's wrong?" Dean placed a gentle hand on her arm.

"He regrets it," she whispered.

"What do you mean?" I asked.

With tears in her eyes, she turned to us. "He said he never should have kissed me. That it was a mistake. He won't talk to me. I've been to The Cellar twice since the ball. Each time he saw me he made an excuse to get more booze or another keg."

"I'm so sorry, sweetie." Hugging Trina guilt gnawed at me. Maybe I shouldn't have urged him on.

"Screw him, Trina. You will find bigger and better." Dean grabbed her in a fierce embrace.

"Thanks. I'm sure you're right. I just thought if something finally happened between us, it would be magic." She looked down. "Guess I just didn't measure up to Dinah."

"That's fucking bullshit!" Dinah stood behind her. "He's a fucking dumbass. Donny needs to get some backbone. You are twice the woman I am. If he can't see that then his cowardly ass can stay away. Asshat!"

"I second that." Honor said.

Honor was carrying chips and dip. She had just walked in when she heard Dinah's rant. I wasn't sure if she even knew what we were talking about, but it made Trina perk up.

I took her provisions out of her hands. She gave hugs to Trina, Dinah, and Dean.

"Are we ready to party?" She asked

"Absofuckinglutely." Dinah pounded the rest of her drink.

"Honor!" Justin walked over from the kitchen.

"Hello, big brother." Her voice was flat. She was still pissed about the ball.

"Where are the kids?" He looked around as if they were hiding.

"I locked them out in the car." Justin stopped and stared at her. "They are with Steve's parents. You really thought I'd leave them out in the car? You're such an asshole."

Honor walked over to our mothers. Trina, Dinah and Dean wandered over to the couch leaving us alone.

"What the hell did I do?" he asked.

"The look you had on your face said you felt Honor would do that. You know damn well she'd never leave Henry or Willa like that." I scolded.

"I know, Cierra. It's just with that guy from the ball I wasn't sure anymore where her priorities are."

"We've gone over this. You are her brother not her mother." Justin nodded. "Now, go make amends before the clock strikes midnight or you aren't getting any next year," I said.

A look of horror crossed his face. He swiftly walked over to his sister.

"Cierra, thank you so much for inviting me." Jonas watched while I straightened the table.

"You are like family, Jonas. Why wouldn't I invite you? Having a good time?"

Silence met me. I looked at Jonas and saw him staring at Dinah. She was actively trying not to look at him.

"Earth to Jonas." I waved my hands in front of his face.

"Huh?"

"Something happen between the two of you."

Jonas opened his mouth to answer when Honor approached us.

"I'm sorry, Cierra, but my brother is an idiot. I'm glad he is your idiot."

I laughed.

"Hey Jonas! Congratulations! I'm really glad the shelter has been saved."

"How did you know?" He asked.

"I was at the ball."

"Yes, but at the ball we hadn't raised enough money to save the shelter."

"Wait a minute! Yes we did. That's what you told me." I said.

"I lied. I didn't want you to think the ball didn't work." Jonas looked at me sheepishly.

"It didn't? Why weren't you honest with me?"

"I had a plan. If we didn't raise enough money, I was going to go to the mortgage company I use and negotiate something. I didn't have to do that though. When I called two days later, they said the mortgage was in good standing. I didn't need to negotiate, beg or plead." Jonas cocked his head at Honor. "So, how did you know?"

Her face flushed. "Darren."

My brow furrowed. "What about Darren?"

She sighed. "Darren was at the ball for the mortgage company. His partner was supposed to go, but he couldn't. That was why his name wasn't on the list. He saw everything we had done to save the shelter. Being partner, he pulled some strings I guess."

"Wow."

"You can say that again, Cierra." Jonas turned toward Honor and said, "I need to thank him."

"You can't right now. He is out of the country."

"When you talk to him next please tell him thank you from me."

"I won't be seeing him." She snapped.

I sighed. "Lord help me with all the stubborn friends I have."

Before they could respond, Justin turned up the volume on the TV. The giant globe was falling slowly.

The countdown had begun.

10 . . .

Justin walked back toward me.

9 ...

His arms wrapped around my waist.

8 ...

"I love you," he said.

7 ...

"I love you too," I whispered to him.

6 ...

"I want to start every year with you." He tucked a loose strand behind my ear.

5 ...

"What are you saying?"

4 ...

Justin pulled away. The world around us vanished.

3 ...

He bent on one knee in front of me and pulled out a box from his pocket. I gasped.

2 ...

He opened it to reveal a key. "Move in with me, Cierra."

1 ...

"Yes!"

He jumped up and kissed me.

This year was going to be a great one.

EPILOGUE

WTR CHRISTMAS PARTY—ONE YEAR LATER

"How the hell did I manage to get dragged to another corporate Christmas party?" I asked Trina.

"You work here now, remember?" Trina adjusted her ugly sweater.

Being the corporate event planner, I was responsible for the party, now. I was absolutely against any crazy theme. With a sigh, I adjusted the elf costume I was forced to wear.

Instead of the ugly Christmas sweater party with lots of alcohol, we made this into a family party. Justin volunteered to be Santa while I was drafted to be his helper elf. All other WTR employees had to wear their ugly sweaters. We were even going to have a contest to pick the best.

Bells started jingling. "That's my cue."

I pasted on a bright smile and took my jingle bell ass over to a stage. We'd recreated the north pole. All it needed was Santa. Justin worked his way through the crowd of cheering kids and parents. When he managed to make it to me, he winked.

"Ok Ms. Jingles, please bring me my first friend." He said in a husky voice.

A little girl was first in line. "What is your name, sweetie?"

"Her name is Olivia." The little boy behind her spoke up.

"Olivia. That is a very pretty name. Are you ready to see Santa?"

She looked past me to Santa. Fear flashed over her features.

"Can I walk with her?" The little boy asked.

"Do you want . . ." I looked to the little boy.

"Scotty."

"Do you want Scotty to walk with you?" She looked from me to the little boy.

"Ok." Her little voice squeaked out.

Scotty grabbed her hand. They walked together. Justin, or Santa rather, picked up the frightened little girl. Scotty stood next to me waiting his turn. Santa talked gently with Olivia coaxing a smile and some words from her. A WTR employee who was also a photographer snapped a couple pictures. Olivia jumped down, grabbed a candy cane from the basket and ran to her waiting parent.

For the next few hours, I escorted child after child.

"Aunt Cierra!" Willa and Henry were the next children.

"Shh . . . remember what we talked about?" I whispered.

Their two heads nodded in unison.

I squatted next to them. "The other kids don't know that Justin and I are Santa's helpers."

"We know and you know what?" Henry asked.

"What?" I took their hands and walked them up to Justin.

"Unkie Justin has a big surprise for you," Willa giggled.

"Willa! Shush!" Henry admonished.

"Sorry," she said sadly.

"It's ok, Willa. Now, go tell Santa what you want."

Henry and Willa took their turns while Honor waited for them.

In the past year, I had grown to love those two little monsters. They were sweet caring kids. Honor did everything to make sure they had a happy life. Their father may be inconsistent, but she was a rock. She was like a sister to me.

The line dwindled finally. I could tell Justin was getting hot and tired. We planned on leaving soon after the last child gave him their list. My elf costume was starting to ride up in uncomfortable places.

All of the children were now in an adjoining room to have milk and cookies. A children's Christmas train movie played on the room's large screen. Squeals of excitement could be heard.

I couldn't hold back my smile.

"Cierra?" I turned toward Justin's voice.

He had taken the beard and hat off. Then he stripped off the red Santa jacket. He stood in front of me with an ugly Christmas sweater and his Santa pants. His sweater said "Won't you be my Ho-Ho-Ho?" with Santa looking over his shoulder wearing just a thong.

"No wonder you were dying. You had a stinking sweater on." I watched as he knelt down and pulled out a black velvet box.

"Cierra Jameson, you are my life. You are quirky, caring, sweet, beautiful and at times your filter is busted. I wouldn't want you any other way. Since I've met you, I have become a better man. I cannot imagine my life without you. Will you marry me?"

He flipped the velvet box open. Inside was a gorgeous diamond solitaire. My eyes looked from the ring to Justin and back.

I must have taken too long because someone yelled from the back, "Answer the poor boy, Cierra."

My head snapped toward the voice. My parents stood near the door to the room where the kids were.

"Cierra?" Justin was shaking.

It hit me. I hadn't answered yet. "Oh. My. God! Yes! Of course, I will marry you. There isn't anyone else I want to spend my life with."

I kissed Justin hard enough that he toppled over pulling me with him.

"Get a room!" Dad yelled.

"Yeah! Make me grandbabies!" Mom yelled. Everyone in the room stared at her. Unfazed, she just shrugged.

"So was this the surprise the kids knew about?" I asked after our kiss.

"Yes. I thought they were going to spill the beans."

I smiled and said, "I like your sweater."

"I figured it all started with an ugly Christmas sweater. You did give me a hard time after all last year." I shoved his shoulder.

He pulled me close, kissing me again.

Who would have thought an ugly Christmas sweater would have brought me so much happiness?

ACKNOWLEDGMENTS

To my friends: I need to thank you all for the encouragement to keep going with a hobby that has turned into so much more.

To my mom: You are the bookworm I am but you still encourage me to write while you steal my new books 😊

To my beta readers: You have helped to hone this story and take it to another level.

To Rosie: Thank you for taking the time to read and proofread this monster. You really are a blessing.

To Heath, Brayden, Sam, and Shalee: Your encouragement and support has meant the world to me. I couldn't have done any of this without all of you.

CPSIA information can be obtained
at www.ICGtesting.com
Printed in the USA
BVHW071301251119
564754BV00007B/532/P